Boss Babe Murder

Jackson Hole Moose's Bakery Not So Cozy Mystery #3

Sue Pepper

DIMICK LANE
PRESS

For my sisters, the ones I was blessed to be born with, E & C, and the one I chose, W.

Content Warning

Aside from the traditional off-page murder in this murder mystery, this book also contains brief mention of suicide, parent death, and adultery.

Chapter One

There was no way it was snowing again. Sadie Moose peered up at the mountain ahead and the low-lying clouds masking its peak.

No. Damn. Way.

For the love, it was April. Sadie heaved a sigh and gripped the steering wheel of her van tighter. This had been the longest winter of her life. Living in Jackson Hole, Wyoming, she was used to winter starting in October and hanging on to surprise them with snow at least once in May, but this one had drug on and on.

Yes, she'd found a body under the first snow of the season just before Halloween. And another in January, actually, at a snowy hot spring. Yikes. That had all been very unfortunate.

But besides that, things were going great. Truly.

Her second-generation family business, Moose's Bakery, was thriving. The flagship location just off Jackson's town square had seen record business over the winter. She'd even won a yet-to-be-aired reality TV show after accepting a challenge to last-minute produce 4,000 cookies to give away for Valentine's Day.

Sadie glanced around the vehicle she was driving, one of two brand new delivery vans that had been her prize. She still couldn't quite believe that luck. No, really, she didn't believe it was luck. Even though the contracts had been vetted by her attorney and insurance agent, so she'd reluctantly signed them at their urging, she still felt there had to be a catch. She wasn't letting it stop her from using the vans, though.

A gentle rain started, and Sadie flipped on the van's windshield wipers.

No, things were going great.

She'd entered a business partnership with her former head barista, Kendall Craig, and Kendall's new fiancé, billionaire land developer Claire Cabot. Together, they'd built two coffee kiosks that served commuters into the Jackson Hole valley, and were working on a third.

Business was booming.

So why was Sadie so...sad?

She gripped the wheel of the van firmly and willed the mist of tears in her eyes to clear. *Get a grip, Moose.* She took a deep, steadying breath.

She wasn't sure what was wrong with her. Okay, that was a lie.

Men were what was wrong with her.

She'd reunited with her childhood best friend and longtime crush, Merritt West, last fall. They'd had a brief but intense affair before Merritt had left the valley again. She'd then run into her former boyfriend, Jake Moreno, in December, and they'd happily fallen back together. And then in February, Jake had found out he had a twelve-year-old daughter he'd never known, and he'd asked for time and space to figure that out. Now Victoria, his long-lost college girlfriend, and Astrid, his daughter, were living with him. Apparently, Sadie and Jake's relationship was officially over.

And Claire and Kendall were planning a different wedding every day as they waffled on what they wanted their big day to look like. Elope to Vegas! Say vows on a helicopter tour of the Tetons! A grand affair with five hundred guests covered by Claire's hometown *Chicago Tribune*! She couldn't keep up with their ideas.

And her best friend Paige was pregnant with her first and due in a few weeks.

The familiar sadness welled inside Sadie again, and she tried to stifle it. She was nearing her final delivery of the day, and this one should be fun. She needed to put on a happy face. Fake it until she made it. She was escaping this stifling winter in —she checked the digital readout on the van's console—four hours. She could make it four hours. Especially since she would get to visit with her college friend, Amy, when she made this last delivery.

Sadie peered at the map displayed on her phone's GPS. She thought she would've made it to the place by now. The road, a narrow strip of asphalt cut out of the side of a mountain, stretched on and on, disappearing behind a tree-and-snow-covered hill in front of her. The view out the passenger window showed the steep drop-off. She hoped she wouldn't meet another vehicle coming down, as there definitely wasn't enough room for two cars on the road, much less her oversized delivery van.

As she crept up the road, the rain started falling harder. It would be snow at the top, no matter how much she wished it wouldn't be. It may be late April, but that didn't matter in the Tetons. She hoped the guests that gathered at the chalet had packed for the weather.

She snorted. They probably hadn't.

She thought about what she knew about Amy's friends. Or her coworkers? Bosses? It was a mystery to her how, exactly, multi-level marketing companies worked. All Sadie knew was that Amy had started selling Glamarosa Clothing a few years ago and had quickly become a top seller. The patterns, constant new styles, and bright colors weren't really Sadie's style. Nevertheless, she'd bought a few items over the years to support her friend, despite her misgivings about the company's high-profile triplet founders, Glenn, Amalia, and Rosalie Valentine.

The uneasy relationship between the siblings had spilled into the media as the company exploded in popularity, largely driven by social media sales by their enthusiastic, uniformly dressed sales representatives. A few not-so-flattering articles had appeared in major news publications in the last few months, and Sadie thought Amy's smile seemed strained lately in her regular Facebook Live sales.

But those weren't Sadie's problems.

She had enough problems.

And she was going to get away from them for awhile. In less than four hours, she'd be on a plane headed on vacation for the first time in years. Her parents were in town to help run the bakery. Kendall was in charge of the coffee kiosks. Tyrone, her chocolate Lab, was under the care of Kamari, another of her baristas that lived in the basement apartment below Sadie's house. Her suitcases rattled around in the back of the van. She'd wrapped up everything so she could go on this trip.

Just one more stop, and she'd be headed to the airport. Her turn finally appeared on the GPS, and she turned up the steep driveway indicated, creeping through the evergreens until she neared the top of the ridge. The rain had, of course, turned to light snow. She pulled to a stop in front a wrought iron and river rock gate, the back of the van fishtailing as she did. She gritted her teeth. She couldn't wait to be off this damn mountain.

She rolled down the window and jabbed at the call button.

After a moment, a voice crackled through the speaker.

"Yes?"

"I'm Sadie Moose, here to make a delivery, and–"

"Pull around to the back." The voice cut her off abruptly, but the gate began to swing open, so Sadie shrugged it off. She could shrug off any number of slights because she was *getting out of here soon*. She still couldn't see the house, the drive climbing further into the trees in front of her.

And she kept driving.

And driving.

Finally, Sadie pulled into the chalet's circular drive, jaw dropping. It was enormous, an elegant river rock and log mansion perched on a rocky outcropping, the Tetons barely visible in the distance through the low clouds and blowing snow. Her stomach curdled at the wealth wrapped up in this occasionally used retreat.

No. She shook herself. This was a favor for an old friend. She could smile and make nice with the Glamarosa crew running the show long enough to drop the bakery boxes. She didn't need to let her disgust shine through. The boxes shifted in the back of the van, reminding her that as much as she disliked the billionaire second homeowners that were ruining her hometown, she still took their money. *No ethical consumption under capitalism.*

As she pulled under the portico, sticky sweet smile plastered on her face, a stern white woman with close-cropped salt and pepper hair and dressed all in black stepped out and motioned Sadie to lower the passenger side window.

"Vendors need to enter through the back," the woman said, looking down her nose at Sadie. Her words were clipped, an accent Sadie couldn't quiet place sharpening her vowels.

Forcing a smile, Sadie said, "Oh, I'm dropping off desserts, but really I'm here to see my friend–"

"Vendors. Need. To. Go. Through. The. Back." The woman enunciated each word.

Sadie bit back an insult and willed her fake smile to stay in place. "Of course," she said. "I'll pull around to the service entrance." She rolled up the window, her finger jamming the button harder than was strictly necessary.

"Like a servant," she muttered under her breath as the woman nodded curtly and stepped back. Sadie gripped the steering wheel tightly as she rolled the van forward. Just one more stop. One more stop and she would be on a plane headed to a sun-drenched, all-inclusive resort to drown her sorrows.

* * *

Sadie was greeted at the back door by a white man with dark hair and a stiff grimace in a tailored chef's coat. He looked vaguely familiar, but Sadie didn't recognize him from town.

"Desserts, right?" The man peeked around Sadie to peer at the parked van and the Moose's Bakery logo emblazoned on the side.

"That's right," Sadie said, quirking an eyebrow. The stack of bakery boxes in her arms should've been a clue.

"Good." The man backed up, waving Sadie through the door. "Dessert's not in my contract. I don't do pastry, and with this weather..."

"It's nasty out there," Sadie agreed, following the man through a back entry into a gleaming commercial kitchen.

"Just put the boxes on that counter." The man pointed to a space between a pile of hotel pans and clean dishes.

Sadie did so. "There's more in the van. I'll grab them. Have room in the fridge?"

The man nodded distractedly. His attention was focused on a pot simmering on the stove.

Sadie walked out, rolling her eyes. *Nobody here was very friendly.*

The snow had turned back to rain. Ugh. Everything was wet and soggy. A mix of mud season and snow season and rain season, and it wouldn't let up anytime soon. Sadie stacked the last of the boxes in her arms and elbowed the van doors closed, walking back into the kitchen shaking rain out of her hair.

The man was still frowning at the pot, a tasting spoon dangling in the air in front of his mouth as he contemplated. Sadie sat the bakery boxes loudly on the counter.

"These need to go in the fridge. Cheesecakes, individual trifles, and a mousse that's meant to be served with the tartlets."

The man dropped the spoon in the sink with a clatter and frowned at her. "Do you have prep–"

Sadie held up her detailed menu, including pictures with proper plating. "Instructions? Of course." He took them from her.

Sadie finally got a look at the name embroidered on his coat and she gulped, her eyes snapping back on the man's handsome face. Square jaw covered in light stubble. Steely gray eyes. Wavy dark brown hair. Signature tattoo of a radish on his muscular forearm. She was in the presence of Chef Gavin Vincent. Recent winner of the long-running elite TV competition, Chef Off. Genius in the kitchen, but kind of an asshole, if his reality TV portrayal was to be believed.

She snapped her jaw closed. She didn't need to act like a star-struck hick, even if she was one.

He was flipping through the instructions. When he looked up at her, his tense features had softened a degree. "These are great," he admitted. "I'm Gavin, by the way." He stuck out his hand.

"Sadie Moose," she squeaked, grasping his hand and trying to memorize how it felt so she could explain it to her friend

Penny, who was as obsessed with the show as she was. They watched it together while shoving junk food into their mouths and harshly critiquing the chef's performances.

His face perked up even more. "Oh, Moose's Bakery, right? I wanted to swing by there while I was in town. I've seen you on TikTok."

Sadie felt her cheeks color. She was often talked into doing trendy dances on TikTok in the name of marketing, and she tried not to think about this heartthrob seeing her doing the latest dance craze. "Oh! That's great! I'm headed out of town after this, but my dad Arlo, who opened the bakery originally, is running it this week."

They were interrupted by the stern-faced woman from outside—the housekeeper? Caretaker? Harbinger of death?—sweeping into the room.

Gavin made eyes at Sadie but pasted on a grin at the woman.

"Still here?" The woman asked, her voice edged with displeasure.

"Have you two met?" Gavin asked, breaking in.

"Actually, no," Sadie said, looking at him gratefully.

The woman's jaw tightened. "I'm Ms. Beatrice. I'm the house manager."

"It's nice to meet you, Ms. Beatrice," Sadie said politely. "I'm Sadie Moose." Sadie cleared her throat. "A friend of mine is here, and we'd made plans to visit before the retreat kicks off. Amy Peters?"

To her credit, Ms. Beatrice kept her emotions off her face. "Ah," she said, a bite to her voice. "Of course. Ms. Peters. I'll let her know you're here."

But she didn't need to, because right then, Amy burst in, squealing. "Moosey moose!"

Chapter Two

When Amy bounded into the kitchen, Sadie felt her familiar energy sweep into the room, and she couldn't help but smile, couldn't help but be buoyed by it.

They'd met on the first day of college orientation, in those frantic moments where friendships are often made and then discarded later when friend groups are organized. But instead of quietly slipping away from one another until they waved across the quad and never spoke again, Amy and Sadie stayed close. Amy was a musical theater major with expressive features, a voice that carried, and boundless exuberance. Sadie was quieter, a business major, and liked to look before she leapt. But their shared love of Broadway and baked goods was too strong of a bond for them to drift apart, and they'd ended up rooming together for the last of their undergrad years.

She caught Amy as she launched herself at her, and the two hugged. She smelled of nail polish, floral perfume, and the mint gum she was often chewing. When Sadie pulled back, Amy stayed close a beat longer, and Sadie felt a tinge of worry. But when Amy finally pulled away, she was smiling, and Sadie saw no cause for concern in her expression.

"Eeek, I'm so happy to see you!" Amy almost sung the words, her body vibrating with excitement. She was taller than Sadie by an inch, which put them both in the short category, but was wearing towering wedge boots, which made Sadie look up at her. She had generous curves and high, round boobs her parents had bought her for college graduation. She was white, and her brown hair was highlighted blonde with that just-blown-out look Sadie associated with women that had time to spend at the salon weekly. Gold jewelry flashed at her wrists, her neck, her ears. Her makeup, including what had to be false eyelashes, was flawless. She was wearing Glamarosa clothing head to toe—a flowy, flowery plaid dress, black leggings, and a tailored jacket. A trendy black flat-brimmed felt hat completed the look.

Sadie blinked at her, taking it all in. Amy had always had to do her makeup before they left the house, even when they were scrubby and only headed to Taco Bell, but this was a more polished, put together version of Amy than she remembered. Sadie felt mousey in comparison. She was wearing joggers stuffed into mud boots and a Moose's Bakery sweatshirt, her brown hair pulled up into a high ponytail. She'd remembered to put on makeup this morning, but as usual, she was sure she probably had mascara smeared around her eyes, darkening them like the bags she knew were underneath. No wonder the woman in black—who was staring at them with hostility—had been so snooty. If everyone here was as well made up as Amy, Sadie would never fit in. Or at least, she'd never fit in without a few hours of pampering first.

"I'm happy to see you too," Sadie said finally, and meant it. She hadn't seen Amy in person for several years. Almost as long as it had been since she'd left the valley for longer than a day trip.

Sadie felt eyes on them and turned to Gavin, who was leaning up against the counter, watching them.

"Gavin, this is my friend Amy," Sadie said.

"Amy," Gavin said, all charm, "a pleasure."

Amy smiled a little coolly back at him and returned the greeting, then turned back to Sadie. "Let's go visit! I want you to see this stunning house!"

Sadie felt Ms. Beatrice watching them as Amy pulled her out the way she'd came, and Sadie peeked down at her boots. She'd kicked the mud off before entering the kitchen, at least.

Amy kept a running commentary as she pulled Sadie through a long hall with many doors coming off it, then into the guest portion of the house. Her trip had been fine. She was glad she'd flown in before the weather hit. Her mom was cat sitting for her. Sadie wouldn't believe the room she'd been assigned on the top floor. She kept going, but Sadie had stopped listening as they entered the large great room. The ceiling soared two stories above them into a high peak, with one wall of the room completely glass, letting in what would be a breathtaking view of the Tetons when it wasn't late-onset spring blizzarding.

A fire roared in the river rock fireplace, real logs piled next to it. No fake gas fires here. The room was broken up into several conversation areas, and Amy pulled her into the one with the coziest looking couches. Sadie took a seat and Amy plopped down next to her, slipping her boots off and tucking her feet under her. Sadie shifted, uncomfortable, then finally took her own boots off and cozied onto the couch.

Amy was still talking.

"—can you believe this room? Isn't it incredible? Glenn, Amalia, and Rosalie rented the chalet for the week. I feel so lucky to be included in their retreat!"

Sadie finally broke in.

"How did you get chosen?"

Amy paused, looking around the empty room furtively before leaning in closer to Sadie. "That's a good question! Normally these things are sales rewards, but this time I was invited and no one else in my sales tier was. You wouldn't believe who else is here! The Joneses, Steffy Austin, Barbie and Ken..." Amy said the names as if Sadie should recognize them, then trailed off when Sadie looked at her with confusion. "Oh, they're rock stars in the Glamarosa world! Steffy Austin earns in the seven figures!"

Sadie blinked at her. She hadn't realized the direct sales clothing business could be that lucrative. She knew Amy did well, but she wasn't selling seven figures...was she? "Is it just relaxing and fun, or are there, like, lectures to attend?"

Amy laughed. "Luckily, Glamarosa meetings are always fun! The program includes a few meetings every day, but we're having a spa day, yoga every morning, and skiing later in the week if we want to go."

"Fun," Sadie said, meaning it. She hoped Amy had a good week. Sadie would be having one too, but instead of skiing, she planned on parking her butt under a beach umbrella and taking advantage of the all-inclusive margaritas and tacos.

"Anyway, that's enough about me. How are you, friend?" Amy glanced over Sadie's lackluster outfit, a crease appearing between her brows.

Sadie grasped for a smile. "I'm doing okay. A bit of a rough winter, but business is booming. I even won that van I drove here in a reality TV show!"

They chatted about Sadie's glimpse at stardom, their families, and their mutual friends for awhile, Sadie eventually relaxing into the easy warmth and banter she and Amy had always enjoyed. They were giggling about a mutual friend's recently posted unfortunate family photos when they were joined in the room by a white couple, the woman sour-faced and the man handsome but blank-faced, following her dutifully. Amy's eyes widened when she saw them, and she stood up, stumbling to get her boots back on.

"I thought the welcome mixer was in here," the woman said, observing Amy distantly.

Amy cleared her throat and glanced at her smartwatch. "Not for another hour, I don't think."

The woman's head snapped towards the man behind her, her perfectly coiffed blonde hair not moving as she did so. That was some hairspray. The man looked panicked, then glared at his own analog watch, blanching.

"Time change, my dear," he said meekly. "We must be ahead of schedule coming from the East coast."

The woman rolled her eyes and stomped further into the room, giving Sadie a chance to take in her full outfit. It was a lot. A short skirt over eighties-patterned leggings, two layered shirts, a long duster vest, jewelry up both arms, more necklaces than Sadie could count, and a hat identical to Amy's, just a different color.

"I love your outfit," Amy said and Sadie glanced at her to see if she was serious. She apparently was, as she looked at the leggings longingly. "I've been trying to find that pattern. And I think we have the same hat."

The woman glanced down at the pants dismissively. "Oh, right. Well, when you order as much product as I do, you eventually see all the prints." She took her hat off and shoved it at the man trailing behind her.

"Of course," Amy said, still smiling. "I'm Amy Peters, by the way."

"I'm Brett. This is my wife, Kenna," the man said, juggling the hat and a purse Sadie imagined belonged to his wife. Kenna stalked towards the windows and frowned, ignoring them. "We're best known as—"

"—Barbie and Ken," Amy finished, laughing. "I'm a fan."

Brett nodded, his cheeks pinkening. "And your friend?"

Sadie felt herself flush. Brett was wearing a well-tailored suit. She was definitely underdressed. "I'm the dessert caterer," she said, pulling on her own boots and standing. "An old friend of Amy's." She checked her watch. Her flight left in two and a half hours. She should get going. "And I was actually just leaving."

"So you're not with Glamarosa?" Kenna had turned away from the windows and was looking at Sadie with a predatory gleam in her eye.

"Oh, nope, I catered the desserts y'all are going to enjoy this weekend. I own a bakery in Jackson."

"A businesswoman! So am I! Have you ever considered adding another revenue stream? Every woman buys clothing, you know. I don't think you can say the same thing about baked goods."

Sadie forced herself to smile and not look at Amy, who she could tell was uncomfortable with her friend being pitched. "That's an interesting proposal. I appreciate you asking," she said, trying to sound sincere, "but I'm happy with my business as is."

"It's recession-proof. Clothes. Especially if women eat too many brownies." Kenna eyed Sadie's rounded figure like she suspected Sadie was guilty of that.

Sadie gritted her teeth. She needed out of here. She opened her mouth to excuse herself but was interrupted as more people came into the room. Amy straightened next to her, taking her arm and squeezing it meaningfully.

Sadie took the cue to keep her mouth shut and stood silently as the group filed in. At the front were the three white, tall, statuesque, dark-haired siblings and cofounders of Glamarosa: Glenn, Amalia, and Rosalie Valentine.

* * *

Sadie had thought Kenna's outfit was over the top, but she needed to rethink her scale as she took in the outfits the company founders were wearing. Glenn was wearing a tailored black suit with a wild-patterned tie and pocket square, his only nods to the clothing line. But next to him, Amalia, or maybe it was Rosalie, they were identical, so it was hard to tell, wore— Sadie counted carefully—seven pieces of Glamarosa clothing. A lacy skirt that peeked out below an A-line dress, leggings, a top layered over the dress, a lace vest, a duster cardigan, and, hold up, another lace vest on top of that. Next to her, her sister wore a slightly less stifling amount of clothes, but the effect was the same. Sadie bit the inside of her cheek to keep from giggling. It made sense for the company founders to take pride in their clothes, obviously. But the layers reminded her of Joey in the episode of Friends when he wore all of his clothes as revenge on Chandler. If that's what they liked, it was good for them, but looking at them made Sadie claustrophobic and sweaty.

Like Amy and Kenna, the two women were perfectly made up, their black hair blown out and falling in waves down their backs, multi-metaled bracelets clacking. Sadie noticed for the first time that Kenna and the two company founders both wore the same necklace—a large rose strung on a delicate chain, leaves along it. Kenna's was rose gold and had fewer leaves strung on the necklace than the company founders. Their necklaces were silver, with gems for leaves. Sadie peeked at Amy, realizing she also wore a rose necklace, gold with numerous gold leaves.

She was puzzling over that when she was suddenly enveloped in a tight, rose-scented hug.

"Hello darling!" The woman, either Rosalie or Amalia, was saying as she wrapped her arms around her. "It's been so long since I've seen you!" She had a light Jersey accent, and Sadie remembered the three were from a large Italian family in New Jersey. Amalia had even had a cameo on the Real Housewives of New Jersey a few seasons ago, setting up an in-home boutique in an echoey faux-Tuscan mansions. Two of the housewives had fought over a pair of skull-patterned leggings, and that footage had gone viral.

Sadie froze in the floral-scented hug. Amy was being wrapped up in a hug by the other sister, and Glenn was giving similar greetings to Barbie and Ken.

The woman pulled back to smile at Sadie, still gripping her by her arms. Her eyes glanced down at her outfit quickly, but her smile never fell.

"How was your trip here? How long has it been?"

Sadie finally unfroze.

"Uh, actually, I'm the dessert caterer, Sadie Moose? I'm friends with Amy."

The woman didn't even blink, just squeezing Sadie's arms again before dropping her long-red-fingernailed hands.

"Oh, of course, I knew I recognized you," she said. "I'm Rosalie Valentine. Thank you so much for being here."

"Happy to," Sadie stammered. Rosalie was wrapping Amy up in a hug and Sadie was being treated to an Amalia hug now. Amalia didn't smell like roses—she smelled of fresh citrus. Sadie wondered if that was the only way to tell the two apart if you didn't know them better.

"Thank you for catering for us," Amalia said, pulling away. "I can't wait to try your concoctions. I've heard so much about you."

Sadie wondered how that could be true, but she was being passed to Glenn, who smiled down at her while wrapping her hand in a firm, two-handed handshake.

Meeting the Valentine's was a full-on sensory experience. They'd entered the room and the excess oxygen had gone out. Sadie could see how they'd successfully built their empire. They made everyone in the room seem special, like they had their full attention. And if they didn't have their attention... Kenna had fallen out of the spotlight of Glenn and was now elbowing Amy aside to get Rosalie's smile beamed at her.

Cutthroat. Sadie felt a shiver on her spine and wanted out. Immediately. She felt bad for Amy, being thrown to these spiders that so carefully wrapped you up in their webs. Not for the first time, she worried about the investment Amy had made in this company, for her leaving her normal nine-to-five job as a music teacher to do this exclusively. She'd even sat out the last season of community theater, her passion, because she was too busy selling clothes.

But Amy was a big girl.

And Sadie had a plane to catch.

She was outta here.

Chapter Three

But before she could exit the room, another group had joined them. At the front was a petite white woman with a cascade of wavy rainbow hair, heavy eye makeup, glitter eyeshadow, and an outfit more punk rock than the other Glamarosa women. She wore one pair of plain leggings, strategically ripped, over a patterned pair.

"Amalia!" the woman cried as Amalia cried, "Steffy!", and she rushed into the woman's open arms. Sadie caught Kenna rolling her eyes, and Amy stiffened, but kept smiling. Behind Steffy, four more people filed in. The first was an Asian couple, the man dressed more casually in khakis and a button down, the woman in the same wildly put together clothes as the other women. They looked a little wide eyed as they took in the house and the gathering. The other two were white women, so close in appearance they must be sisters, one with a petulant look on her face, red lips tilted down, the other with a pasted-on grin, overly large white teeth blinding.

"Friends!" Rosalie moved forward, smiling, edging Amalia and Steffy aside as they stood, heads together, whispering.

Amalia's smile looked strained as Steffy jabbered at her insistently.

Sadie glanced at Amy, who nodded at her, and they slipped around the gaggle of extravagantly dressed, highly scented flamingoes strutting for one another. Amy followed her back the way they'd come.

Gavin was plating appetizers when they entered the kitchen and frowned up at them. "I'm supposed to have an assistant, you know," he complained, spraying something from a metal canister on top of a canapé.

Sadie winced. "They're probably stuck at the bottom of the hill in this storm."

Gavin's frown intensified. "They better get here soon. I can't cater a party of thirty by myself."

Sadie wished him luck and turned to Amy to give her a hug goodbye.

If she imagined Amy squeezed her a little longer than was necessary, she shrugged it off. Again. Amy was a big girl. She'd gotten herself into this. She could get herself out of it if she wanted to. And what had Sadie really seen that was so bad? Competitive spirit? Overly friendly people? Sadie looked into Amy's eyes as she said goodbye.

"You're going to be okay, right?" She asked.

A flurry of emotions overtook Amy's face. "Yeah," she said, her voice strained. "I'm so excited to be here."

"Okay." Sadie opened the back door, having to push it harder than seemed necessary, then peered out at the weather. She hoped the van would make it down the mountain okay. She just needed to get to the airport. Kendall was going to come pick up the van later.

She waved goodbye to Amy one last time, then walked toward her van, feeling lightweight outside, away from the tension inside the chalet, even with the wintry mix of rain and snow pelting her.

She stepped over a large crack in the asphalt, wondering if it had been there when she'd walked in. She hadn't noticed it. That was strange. Sadie paused, her senses telling her something was happening. Her van was only feet away. Down the drive, she could see another van approaching. Were the trees, there on the road below, tilting at a strange angle? She squinted, her brain not able to understand what her eyes were seeing.

The ground rumbled. An earthquake?

A sound like a freight train rolling by filled the air, followed by an unearthly slumping sound, the sound of dumping a bucket of wet mud, except magnified to be the loudest, most unnerving sound she'd ever heard.

Sadie ducked instinctually, not entirely sure what was happening. The ground shook again. The noise intensified, this time filled with the sound of trees breaking, rocks moving, the ground rearranging itself.

In front of her eyes, the van headed up the drive vanished, along with half the mountainside.

Then there was silence. Except for the screams.

* * *

Sadie was running before she'd put together what happened in her head.

She heard footfalls behind her and realized she wasn't the only one rushing down the slippery drive towards the calamity her brain was still identifying.

Landslide.

Across the valley, almost 100 years ago, one of the largest landslides in geological history had cut off the Gros Ventre River, spurred on by heavy rains on top of record snowpack and the unique geological makeup of the area mountains. While no one had died in the landslide, the earthen dam formed by the cut-off river failed a few years later, flooding the town of Kelly downstream and killing six. Sadie had known the story her whole life. She saw the scar of the landslide regularly, the slump still visible across the valley and marked by an interpretive trail at the site. But even with that reminder of the wild power of nature in her mind, she couldn't believe what she'd seen.

Her boot slipped on snow and she almost fell, but a strong hand grabbed her, keeping her upright. Chef Gavin was steadying her, and once she was steady on her feet again, he sprinted in front of her. Five yards beyond them, there was nothing. No road. No van.

But there were shouts from the gaping maw where there was once asphalt road.

Gavin stopped short, throwing out an arm to prevent her from rushing past him.

"It's unstable here," he said unnecessarily. The ground shifted beneath her feet. Every instinct within her screamed to run back to the house.

"Can you see the van?"

He shook his head grimly.

"Help!" A loud shout came from the breach.

Sadie swallowed hard. "We're here!" She yelled back.

"There's three of us. The van's stuck on a tree, but we can't get out!"

"We'll help you. Stay still!" Sadie yelled back.

She felt Gavin's eyes on her, heard his intake of breath when she promised they would help them.

"We have to," Sadie said resolutely. Gavin stared at her, his gray eyes piercing. After a moment, he nodded.

"You're right." He looked around, searching for solutions.

Sadie could see people running down from the house. The screaming had abated. She hoped someone had called 911.

"Here," a voice said from behind them. A length of rope was pushed in front of their faces, and Sadie followed the hand holding it up a tailored suit arm to find Glenn, panting hard, pocket square askew, face red.

Gavin reached for the rope and started to wrap it around his waist. Sadie wanted to insist she go instead, but Gavin was a foot taller than her and weighed less. If anyone should go, it should be him. Sadie could help anchor the rope.

With very few words uttered between them, Glenn, Sadie, and two more men in suits that had run from the house lined up, gripping the rope, feet planted firmly on the ground. Gavin took a deep breath, then stepped carefully towards the edge. When he reached it, he leaned over, using their hold on the rope to get a good look at what was going on.

"They're about ten feet down!" He shouted. "I'll have to go over the edge!"

"Man," the guy behind Sadie said lowly. "This is a bad idea. We should wait for search and rescue." He had a Jersey accent too.

"They probably can't fly in this weather," Sadie said. A light snow was still flying, the wind picking up and reducing visibility. "It'll take time to come from town, and they can't even see where they'd have to stop. Can you see the other side of the road?"

There was a grumble behind her, but the man didn't complain any more.

They'd slowly let out enough rope that Gavin disappeared over the edge. Sadie's heart was pounding so loud she could hear it in her ears. This could go wrong any second. They could lose their grip on the rope. They could be unable to pull Gavin plus the weight of whoever he was trying to rescue back up. The ground could be swept out from underneath them, carrying them all down the mountain in a brutal crush of rock and soil and trees and snow.

But they had to try.

A new sound behind them, this time mechanical, and a large black truck backed up to them. The driver hopped out, and Sadie was surprised to see Ms. Beatrice herself was the driver.

"Hook the rope to the truck," she instructed, and after a slight pause, the man in back moved to do so, the other three on the rope continuing to hold the weight of Gavin. Ms. Beatrice supervised the knot he tied to the back hitch, and after giving it a good tug, motioned for them to step away from the rope.

It was hard for Sadie to let go, both because she was worried she would drop the brave chef, and because her hands seemed frozen in position. They were wet, and cold, and her palms burned. But eventually she uncurled them, gingerly letting the weight go, letting out a big sigh of relief when she realized the truck was easily holding the weight.

The five of them stood around, unsure what to do next, and then Gavin yelled. "I've got one climbing up!"

"Get down there and help them," Ms. Beatrice snapped.

Glenn and the other two men looked at each other warily and didn't move, so Sadie left them behind and followed the harsh woman's orders. It was the right thing to do. Her, Gavin, and Ms. Beatrice were not with Glamarosa. She felt like they were on the same team. Ms. Beatrice was supervising the hitch and the truck in case she needed to drive away, Gavin was doing the saving, and Sadie would help. Glamarosa would do what Glamarosa would do.

Cautiously, Sadie followed the rope to the edge, peering down below. A head popped up, and Sadie held out a hand to the white-faced man with a large black backpack who had climbed up the slope using the rope. He took it, and Sadie pulled hard, both of them collapsing back onto the road. The man quickly rolled away and scurried up the driveway, trying to put as much room as possible between him and the danger he'd just barely escaped.

"Second one headed up!" Gavin yelled, and Sadie scrambled back to her feet to peer over the edge again. Now that she was feeling braver, and the ground wasn't moving beneath her feet, she was able to see what was going on down the slope. The white van, very similar to her delivery van, was caught on a spruce tree root. The trees had shallow but wide root systems, luckily for the people in the van. When the road had collapsed underneath them, they'd slid down before finally stopping against the roots, upside down. The windows of the van were smashed in. Gavin had picked his way down the slope to grab people out through the front window. A second man, also wearing a big black backpack—what commitment to their belongings, Sadie would've left everything behind—was about ten feet away from her. Gavin had his hand out and was helping one more man through the broken windshield.

The man reached Sadie, and she held out a hand to help him up. He had suffered multiple cuts and had a blossoming bruise on his cheek. He looked dazed. His grip was firm though, and Sadie pulled backwards to haul him up as she had the first man. He came up easily, collapsing next to her.

"This man needs medical attention!" Sadie shouted up the slope, her eyes taking in the scene behind her for the first time. They'd drawn a crowd. Sadie didn't see Amy, but she saw one of the Valentine sisters, and Barbie and Ken, and the Asian couple that had been introduced as the Bautistas. The first man was being checked over by Leo Bautista, who she'd heard was a doctor. The other two men that had helped with the rope were holding the crowd back and watching the rope while Ms. Beatrice sat inside the truck, ready to rev it up if needed.

"Last one headed your way!"

Sadie twisted her gaze back to the van, seeing a white man with brown hair, a black backpack, and a large duffle working his way up the slope towards her. Sadie hoped there was gold, or diamonds, or something else as valuable in those bags, the way they all insisted on bringing them up.

When the man reached her, she reached out her hand to him. His eyes met hers, and her breath caught. She knew this man. She knew his short-cropped brown hair, now shot through with gray. She knew his clear blue eyes, his square jaw covered in a short beard. And she knew the touch of the strong hand in hers as he clasped it, his eyes suddenly guarded. Why was he here, of all places? Now? As Sadie shifted her weight back to haul him up, a look of panic flitted across his features, and Sadie wondered why.

Then she felt the ground give way beneath her feet.

Chapter Four

Sadie hated rollercoasters. The dread of the climb, the pitch of her stomach at the drop, the screams all around her.

But rollercoasters had nothing on the feeling of the ground giving way beneath your feet, knowing you were falling through the air, with no one to catch you, your scream the last thing anyone would hear from you before you were buried beneath a mountain of earth forever.

Until she was caught by Glenn Valentine, a bruising grip around her ankle. And her hand tightened on the man's, refusing to let him go.

More hands grabbed her, and she was hauled back onto the firm surface of the driveway, the man right alongside her. The world was shouts and snow on her face and her ankle burning with pain. She heard the truck engine roar, and the rope hauling Gavin moved nearby. She hoped he was okay.

She turned her head towards the man from her past, who lay beside her, breathing heavily.

His eyes met hers.

"Here," he said in a low, serious voice, "my name is Nick Walker."

Sadie shook her head to clear it. Was she imagining things? "What?"

"I'm serious, Sadie. You don't know me, and my name is Nick Walker."

Then they were being pulled to their feet and hustled towards the house. Gavin was back, bruised and dirty, his chef's coat ripped, but walking gingerly. He raised an eyebrow at her as she limped back to the house, her mind whirling with what Adam, her study buddy and occasional hookup from grad school, could be talking about. And then she noticed the cameras.

*   *   *

They convened in the great room, blankets distributed by Ms. Beatrice wrapped around the shoulders of those who had been outside. Sadie sat next to Amy on the same couch they'd sat on just an hour before, gossiping. She shivered under the blanket, her clothes soaked and dirty. The fire had been built up, candles brought into the room to illuminate it.

The power was out, but evidently it would be temporary. The house had a generator.

The faces gathered in the room were drawn, serious. Tears streaked Amalia and Rosalie's faces. Glenn stood near them, his fancy suit covered in mud and ripped from where he'd dove to save Sadie. She needed to thank him for saving her life.

Amy had her arm wrapped around Sadie, squeezing her tightly. She'd run out just as they'd reached the kitchen doors. Apparently, Rosalie had been hysterical, so she'd stayed inside to comfort her instead of coming out to help save the men in the van.

Speaking of them. The contents of the black bags and cases they'd insisted on carrying up the slope had become clear to her. This was a film crew, she'd been informed by Amy. They were shooting a documentary about Glamarosa. And apparently, the calamity that they'd just survived was going to be included. Sadie studied Adam where he stood behind the camera operator, the Hispanic man she'd helped first, refusing to meet her eyes. Sadie had looked for a flicker of recognition in Amy's face when he'd walked in the room, but she hadn't shown any. Thinking back, Amy might never have met Adam in college. She'd been working several hours away after graduation, and Sadie's grad school friends hadn't mixed much with her and Amy's group of friends. Sadie again wondered what his game was, but her spiraling thoughts were interrupted by Ms. Beatrice bustling back into the room.

She glanced around, making sure everyone was present, before launching into her announcements.

"I've contacted the authorities. Unfortunately, the weather means they can't rescue us now. We're meant to just sit tight until they can get here."

"And when will that be?"

"What if the chalet slides off the hillside in the meantime?"

"This is outrageous!"

Ms. Beatrice held out her hands to quell the objections of the group. "The rain has turned to snow. It seems likely the mountain is done sliding."

"Can we walk out a different way?" This from Ken.

"Or ski?" This from a handsome young man who was standing close to Steffy.

"It's a sheer cliff above us," Ms. Beatrice said. "If you brought skis, you might be able to ski out below us–"

"That would be incredibly dangerous in these conditions,"

Sadie cut in. "The avalanche danger is high with the rain on all this snow."

"So now we need to worry about an avalanche?" Amalia wailed, her eyes beginning to water again.

"Most likely not," Ms. Beatrice said, cutting a harsh look at Sadie, who shrugged. What she said was true. "Though I do agree with Ms. Moose's assessment. This storm is supposed to continue for the next twenty-four hours or so. We'll have the power back on soon, and we'll be able to host you as you'd planned."

Kenna made a disgruntled noise, but Glenn nodded. "That's what we'll do, then. We'll just carry on as normal as best we can. The retreat has become a true retreat." He sounded amused. Sadie wasn't amused.

She cleared her throat. "Um. I'm not supposed to be here."

He blinked at her. "Right. Well, looking around, it looks like not everyone made it up the mountain." He sobered. "Has anyone heard from those that were invited?"

People checked their phones for text messages, realizing quickly that they had no cell service.

"When the power comes back on, the Wi-Fi will work," Ms. Beatrice assured everyone. "Get me the names of who's missing, and I'll contact the sheriff to check in on them through the satellite phone. They're closing the road, so we don't have to worry about anyone finding their way up here on accident."

Glenn turned his attention back towards Sadie. "We have spare rooms, is what I was trying to say. You are welcome here as a guest." He cleared his throat. "Additionally, I must thank you and Gavin," he gestured at the chef, "for your tremendous bravery in saving our documentarian friends. You acted quickly and without regard for your own safety. True heroes. Gavin, we can upgrade your room as well."

"I want to stay near the kitchen, but thank you," Gavin said, nodding in recognition of their gratitude.

Everyone murmured their thanks, and Amy squeezed Sadie tighter. Sadie felt herself blush. She couldn't imagine reacting any other way. That Amy, or Amalia, or Kenna, or Steffy, or Rosalie, or anyone else in the room hadn't been right next to her, made no sense to her.

"Uh, same," she said finally, smiling at Glenn. "You saved me and A—Nick."

He nodded at her. "I'm very grateful. Thanks be to the Lord." He made the sign of the cross, then took a deep breath. "Okay. Let's all take time to get resettled in our rooms, then we'll come back here to eat and share news in an hour. Will that work? Gavin?"

Gavin shrugged. "Without an assistant, nothing will be as fancy as we'd planned, but I can feed you."

"I'm sure whatever you make will be delicious. Oh, and Sadie," he added as everyone stood and started filing out of the room, "we will need you to sign a film release. Nick will get you the information."

"Right," Sadie said, eyeing her old friend, who was still resolutely refusing to meet her eyes. "Of course."

Ms. Beatrice was next to her then. "I'll show you to a room," she said, her voice a fraction warmer than it had been.

"Oh, and we'll get you some clothes!" Amy said, looking to Glenn. "We probably have some Glamarosa for her, right?"

Sadie waved her off. "I actually have a suitcase in the car. I was headed to Mexico after this, remember?"

Amy winced. "I'd forgotten."

Sadie heaved a sigh. "I hadn't." She glanced at her watch. Her plane would leave without her in twenty minutes. "I'll get my suitcase, and then I'd love to get cleaned up in my room."

Ms. Beatrice nodded at her.

Glenn stopped her. "We'll still get you some Glamarosa. As a thank you. We always travel with stock. Amy, will you pick out things for her? Rosalie and Amalia can help."

Sadie bit back a protest. They were just trying to be nice. And at least if Amy picked things out, she'd make sure everything would fit her.

"Thank you," Sadie said politely, then made her way down the twisty hallway towards the kitchen.

* * *

She entered the kitchen and came to an abrupt stop.

Gavin stood at the counter, arms braced against it, his muscled biceps straining as he gripped hard, his head down, eyes closed as he breathed rapidly. Sadie gulped, trying to decide if she should flee or try to comfort him.

"I know you're there," he said, making the decision for her. He didn't open his eyes or loosen his grip.

"Are you okay?" He didn't answer.

She saw him try to control his breaths, saw the color draining from his face, and realized what was going on. It was shocking she herself wasn't in the midst of a panic attack, after what had just happened. Hers would probably come later, in the dark of her room, when the feeling of her body falling through space would hit her again and again. Thank God she'd packed for a vacation and her anti-anxiety meds were accessible to her.

Slowly, she stepped closer to him. She put her hand down next to his. Not on it, but close to it. "Do you know box breaths? I can do them with you. It's good to grip onto this sturdy butcher block. It can hold you here as long as you need it. I'm going to breathe in for four, then hold it for four, then breathe out for four, if you want to try to do it with me."

She did one round of breaths, and on the second round, he joined her. She put her hand alongside his, so just her pinky touched his thumb, and he loosened his grip on the table, letting his hand relax against hers. They continued to breathe together.

When he opened his eyes minutes later, Sadie smiled at him. "Let's find a place to sit for a minute, and I'll get you some water."

She found a chair in the back pantry and led him to it. He didn't protest. She grabbed a bottle of water from the fridge and brought it to him, unsure if the plumbing would work without the power on yet.

He held it to his forehead for a long moment before taking a drink.

"Can I get you anything else? Do you have meds somewhere?"

His eyes flashed to hers, and she shrugged. "Takes someone with anxiety to recognize someone with anxiety," she said softly.

"I think I'm good, actually," he said finally. "Thank you. For your help just now, and for earlier. That was...that was a lot."

"You were brave," Sadie said. "I just followed your lead. Did you hurt yourself when the rope tightened on you?"

He felt his side. "It's a little tender, but I didn't break any ribs or anything. I'll be okay. Dr. Bautista checked me out earlier."

"Are you really up for feeding all these people?"

He let out a short laugh. "It's what I do. I'll make it work."

"I can help. I worked for a caterer in college, and I know my way around a professional kitchen."

He smiled at her then, the first real one he'd pointed at her, and Sadie felt the full power of the personality he'd leveraged to win over the judges on Chef Off. "I might take you up on that. But for now, you should get settled. I'm going to rest a few minutes, then I'll get food together."

"Okay. But we should stick together. Everyone here is Glamarosa, except for us."

"And Ms. B."

"Right. And Ms. B. And the documentarians."

"But they were hired by Glamarosa, so I wouldn't count on them to be on your side," he said, and she frowned at him.

"What's that mean?"

He shrugged. "Nothing. Just. Watch your back. And what you say."

Then he stood, headed for the kitchen, and Sadie watched his back as he did. He'd changed into a new chef's coat and run a comb through his hair. Sadie wondered for the first time how disheveled she looked, and winced, looking at her muddy, ripped clothes. She couldn't wait to change. Maybe the water would come back on, and she could think about what Gavin had meant while she washed the last hour's worth of activity off of her.

Chapter Five

The power was on when Sadie walked back into the kitchen. Gavin was nowhere to be seen, but Ms. Beatrice was waiting for her. For all she'd rushed to help with the film crew rescue, not a hair was out of place. Her stern expression was back.

"Follow me," she said curtly, and Sadie did so, leaving her mud boots by the back door.

They went back through the long hallway, then turned to go up the wide staircase, going up one flight. The stairway continued up to the right to the next floor. In front of them was a sitting room, bookshelves along the back wall, chairs scattered about. The hall split to the left and right, rooms situated along it in a horseshoe shape.

"The biggest rooms are in the middle, behind the sitting area, in the U of the horseshoe. You're in a junior suite, just here."

Ms. Beatrice turned left, down the dim hallway. "The lights are on emergency power, so it'll be a little dark in the common areas. We'll ask that you keep your energy use to a minimum.

Showers are fine if kept short, but please no hair dryers or other things that pull a lot of power."

"Of course," Sadie said. "Are you from Jackson, Ms. Beatrice?"

The woman was quiet for a long moment. "I'm originally from Germany, but I've managed this chalet for the absentee owners for the last two years."

"Oh," Sadie said, finally placing the accent that clipped her words. "I haven't seen you around town."

"I don't leave much," the woman shrugged. "This place is booked for retreats almost year-round. I don't keep staff, just day laborers when needed. I stay busy."

"Ah." *Control freak*, Sadie thought not unkindly. Sadie liked to manage everything, too, though she'd been better about it lately.

"The Joneses didn't make it, so you'll be in the Rockchuck suite."

Sadie followed behind Ms. Beatrice, her squeaky-wheeled suitcase rolling along noisily behind her on the gleaming hardwood. She peeked at the discreet signs on each door. Albright. Winter. Owen. Teewinot. The suites were named after the mountain peaks in the Teton range. Clever.

Ms. Beatrice stopped abruptly and used a key from the ring that jangled at her waist to unlock the door. "I need to track down the key that we had set aside for the Joneses. I'll have it to you by dinner." She stood aside to let Sadie in, and Sadie inched by her to take in the room. She turned to thank Ms. Beatrice, but the door closed, and Sadie was alone.

The Joneses must be big sellers, because the room was large with a view of the Tetons. Or at least, it would have a view of the Tetons when the snow let up, and it wasn't dark outside. Sadie left her suitcase by the door to explore, her stocking feet sinking into the cushioned cream-colored carpet. It was thick enough she felt like she'd leave footprints as she walked.

The log-frame bed was king size, with an oil painting of Rockchuck Peak above it. Sadie recognized the work as a local artists. Her hand trailed along the bedding. Luxury down and crisp white sheets with a thread count higher than her bank balance. Seven pillows, including one shaped like an actual rockchuck, or yellow-bellied marmot. It shouldn't have been cute, but somehow it was. Sadie named it Flower.

The walls were flat logs, shiny knotty pine that made her miss her bakery. Aside from the bed, there was a sitting area by the window, a bureau, and a walk-in closet that adjoined the bathroom.

The suite she'd booked at the all-inclusive Grand Los Cabos had featured an infinity soaking tub on the balcony, a splurge she'd paid for with long-hoarded credit card points. When the mountain had slumped down, she'd kissed her plans of drinking tequila in that tub overlooking crashing waves goodbye.

But this bathroom, with the soaking tub, rainfall steam shower, and heated marble floors? It would do. She just wished she'd packed tequila in her suitcase. But, hey. Maybe there would be drinks at dinner. Maybe she'd be able to get out of here tomorrow, catch another flight. Which reminded her, she needed to call the airline and the hotel, get her plans pushed back if she could.

But all that could wait until after her shower.

* * *

Thirty minutes later, freshly showered and dressed, Sadie frowned at her reflection in the walk-in closet mirror, then forced herself to stop, watching the line between her eyebrows deepen. Did she want to be the woman with a permanent frown line? She'd rather be like Jake, with permanent wrinkles around his eyes that showed he was usually smiling. *Ugh. Jake.* What was he up to right now? Hanging out with Victoria and Astrid in his cozy cabin, watching the wood stove? Catching up on thirteen years of missing each other over one of Jake's ubiquitous cups of tea? The image in her head of the reunited couple, cozied on the couch, snow falling outside, precocious daughter reading on the rug in front of the fire, rivaled a Norman Rockwell painting. She gritted her teeth and stomped over to the window to peer out.

The wall of earth that blocked the road taunted her. There were no emergency vehicles in sight. The rain had turned to snow, and she cast her eyes towards the Tetons, wondering if she could see the lights of the airport, of the plane she was supposed to be on, but she couldn't. It was coming down thick out there. A late spring blizzard on the heels of a major landslide. She wasn't getting out of this anytime soon. She might as well enjoy it. The kitchen had smelled good earlier, and Gavin was nice to look at. She'd thought they'd shared a real connection, earlier. She looked forward to helping him in the kitchen, getting to know him better. Plus, Sadie knew the desserts on the menu were to die for. Though hopefully no one would be dying.

And she needed to figure out what was going on with Adam. He was playing some sort of game. The words Gavin had said, to watch her back and watch what she said around the documentary crew, came back to her. Something wasn't quite right at this retreat. Maybe figuring out what it was would keep her occupied until she could get out of here. With the power back on, she'd managed to get through to the airline and the hotel. The airline had re-booked her ticket for two days from now, and the hotel was pushing back her reservation. If she ended up having to cancel, her travel insurance would have her covered, but she didn't want to do that.

She'd sent messages to Kendall, Kamari, and her dad, assuring them she was fine, just stuck up at the chalet for now. They'd expressed relief, having heard about the landslide in town. She'd promised to check in again with them later.

Her stomach growled. It was past time for dinner.

Resolved, she took a deep breath and turned back towards the mirror. Her bright, flowy tank dress couldn't be more out of place in this weather, but it was the nicest thing she'd brought. The top scooped low to show her impressive cleavage, and the lightweight fabric floated around her, showing tantalizing generous curves as she walked. The strappy gold sandals were a joke with snow flying outside, but really, what about this scenario wasn't?

Her auburn hair was wet, having honored Ms. Beatrice's request for no hair dryers, so she'd pulled it back in a French braid, then coiled the tail up in a bun at her nape and pinned it up. It was fancier than her normal messy bun, even if it wasn't the fancy blowouts the other women were rocking. Her face was heart shaped, her complexion pale, with a smattering of freckles over her nose. She'd hoped to add natural bronzer from the Mexico sun, but that wasn't going to happen now. She'd gone light on makeup, darkening her eyebrows and lengthening her lashes with mascara, and her green eyes stood out in the paleness of her face. She'd taken out her contacts, a new accessory her mean optometrist had forced upon her last month after she'd resisted glasses for years, and wore a pair of wide round tortoise-shell glasses Kamari said were hip, but Sadie felt a little ridiculous in.

She forced a smile, then relaxed her face and forced another one, this time satisfied she looked less unbalanced. Her teeth were straight, except for the bottom two due to lax retainer-wearing as a teenager. Her smile was a little crooked, just like her nose. She struck a pose, hand on her hip, shoulders back. And rolled her eyes at herself. After the day she had? This would do.

Chapter Six

Sadie heard the buzz of voices in the great room and took a deep breath before sweeping into the room.

Food had been laid along a long sideboard table, and her stomach growled again as she took it in. A bar cart was setup near the fireplace, and she felt gratitude this wasn't a booze-less party. From a podcast on multi-level marketing companies Sadie had listened to, she knew many of them were founded by members of the Church of Jesus Christ of Latter-day Saints, who usually abstained from alcohol.

But not the Valentines. Old school Italians, she saw the three siblings had full glasses of red wine clutched in their hands.

Amy popped up next to Sadie. "You look so cute!" She exclaimed.

"Oh, thanks," Sadie said, looking over Amy's new outfit, a slightly less flashy black sheath dress under a rhinestone-encrusted bomber jacket. "You, too."

"Ms. Beatrice was going to deliver the box of Glamarosa we picked out for you to your room," Amy said. She glanced around.

"Thank you for that," Sadie said. "I didn't see it yet."

"Well, if you want to change eventually..."

Sadie did a double take.

"What?"

Amy bit her lip and glanced around. "It's kind of bad form to be at a Glamarosa party and not wear Glamarosa clothes," she whispered.

"I'm not even supposed to be here," Sadie said, a little too loudly.

Amy put a hand on her arm. "I get it, totally. But you're my guest, so it would make my life easier if you blended in."

Sadie softened. She'd realized how cutthroat this group was earlier. Whatever she could do to make Amy's life easier. "I get it," she said gently. "I need to eat something, then I'll go change. I'm sure you picked out cute stuff."

"Totally," Amy said, breathing out a sigh of relief. "Let's get food, and I'll introduce you to everyone else."

* * *

Gavin was a masterful chef.

Sadie wasn't surprised he'd beaten out the stiff competition in the last season of Chef Off. She'd filled her plate with tender beef roast with a savory wine sauce, perfectly crispy roasted Brussels sprouts with bacon, horseradish whipped potatoes, and a variety of canapés she couldn't quite identify but enjoyed every bite of anyway. As her and Amy ate, plates balanced on their knees where they sat near the roaring fire, Sadie still trying to fight the chill that'd crept into her bones during the rescue, Amy pointed out everyone in the room Sadie hadn't been introduced to yet.

All total, ten people hadn't made it up to the chalet before the road closed. Gavin had said he was cooking for thirty, and Sadie counted less than twenty in the room.

For sellers, there was Amy, Brett and Kenna, aka Barbie and Ken, Steffy Austin, the wide-eyed couple, Leo and Lexi Bautista, and the sisters, Shayna and Julie McCoy.

With the company were the triplets, along with Amalia and Rosalie's husbands, who were the other two men that had helped with the rope, Jonathan and Freddy, and their lead designer, a bald white man who went by Titus. Amalia and Jonathan's son, Jon Jr, was Glamarosa's VP of Retailer Relations. He stuck close to Steffy, which made Amy frown for a reason Sadie didn't know. The company's head legal counsel, Paul Glass, was also there, devouring cocktail shrimp while frowning at the art on the walls.

And then, of course, there was the documentary crew. The camera operator, Alex, and the boom operator, an older white man named Sam, filtered throughout the room, getting footage of the event. It was awkward, and Sadie wondered about the nature of the documentary they were filming. Gavin had said the company had hired them. Was this some sort of company publicity film? One of the many questions Sadie would ask Adam if she could ever corner him.

Sadie's thoughts were interrupted by the sound of cutlery on crystal as Glenn stood on a chair, getting everyone's attention.

"My Glamaristas, I'd like to propose a toast," he boomed. "My sisters and I are so happy to have everyone gathered here. We've gathered sellers from across our leadership levels, those that have been able to change their lives for the better as well as the lives of the teams they lead. We're here to listen to them, learn from them, and have them guide how Glamarosa moves forward into the future, how we reach more and more families. How we bring more and more husbands home!"

There were cheers in the room, and Sadie wondered exactly what that meant.

"Speaking of, Kenna has brought Brett home!"

Everyone cheered then, including Amy. Lexi and Leo Bautista looked uncomfortable. Sadie would have to ask Amy later what that meant in MLM speak.

"After our unsettling afternoon, I also want to raise my glass to our guest, Sadie Moose. She acted bravely today, and we're happy to have her here. As a successful businesswoman, we're sure we'll have a lot to gain from her insight in our general sessions."

Sadie was blushing under the eyes of the room and she realized suddenly why Amy had asked her to go change. The women in the room were eyeing Sadie's non-Glamarosa dress critically. She should've at least run upstairs to throw on a cardigan from their brand or something.

"And finally, I want to address the elephant in the room."

Sadie glanced around. There was an elephant?

"I know there have been rumors, and some disgusting press articles, about distress between me and my sisters." The Valentine sisters looked up at Glenn adoringly. Sadie realized Amalia and Rosalie wore their hair parted on different sides. Aha. A way to tell them apart. "But nothing could be further from the truth. We built Glamarosa together, and we will continue to run it together. After all, Amarosa doesn't have much of a ring to it."

The room laughed.

"Or Glrosa!" Amalia laughed.

"Or Glama!" Rosalie giggled.

"Glama sounds pretty great, actually," Kenna snarked quietly. The Valentines either didn't hear her, or pretended not to.

"So, a toast—to Glamarosa! It's been a roller coaster five years, and here's to the next fifty!"

Everyone clinked glasses and went back to their conversations. Sadie had about a million questions to ask Amy, but she was in discussion with Lexi, so she couldn't. She finished her plate, then sidled up to Glenn, who had hopped off the chair to get a wine refill.

"What's with the documentary crew, if you don't mind me asking?"

Glenn took a gulp of his wine. "Isn't it wonderful? They approached us wanting to do a special on the rise of Glamarosa. They've been following us around for a few weeks now."

"Hm," Sadie mused. "They'll have some exciting footage from today. You know, I was just on a reality TV show."

"Oh really?"

Sadie filled Glenn in on the details, which he at least pretended to be interested in.

"I hired Chef Gavin because I saw him on Chef Off," Glenn said when Sadie was finished with her story. "It can be a real jumping off point for your career. Amalia was on the Real Housewives a few seasons ago and our business increased exponentially afterwards."

"And of course, I was on Next Fashion Star," said a new voice behind them, and they both turned to see Steffy standing there, sipping an amber-colored liquid in a rocks glass and smirking.

"I didn't know that," Glenn said. "How interesting! It's good that we have you working on this design project with Titus, then."

"What season?" Sadie asked, trying to place the rainbow-haired punk rock Steffy. Of course she'd watched all the seasons of Next Fashion Star, most recently as a binge watch during the pandemic when the bakery had been forced to close temporarily.

Steffy shrugged. "I was only in the initial casting but made it on camera. I was asked to return for a subsequent season, but my Glamarosa business was rocking and rolling, so I declined."

Amalia joined them, an empty glass of wine in her hand, the rim smudged red from her lipstick.

"Oh, Amalia," Steffy said, her smile sharp, "I was just telling them about when I was on Next Fashion Star."

Amalia's face went blank, her smile brittle. "Oh?" Her voice was higher than normal, her grip on the wine glass so strong Sadie was worried she might break it.

She was about to ask her what was wrong, but Adam appeared at her elbow.

Sadie tried to play it cool, taking a last sip of her wine.

"Hi," Adam said, clearing his throat. "I need Sadie to sign a film waiver."

"Sure, Nick," Sadie said, emphasizing the name heavily. "Let's go find a place to sign it."

"I have it right here," he held out a piece of paper.

Sadie put her glass down on the nearest table. "I have some questions. I might text it to my lawyer. I never sign anything without legal counsel."

"Smart girl," Glenn intoned.

"Let's go find a quieter place," Sadie insisted.

"This isn't–"

Sadie cut him off by standing and walking out of the room. Sadie felt Amy's eyes on her, but ignored her. She wanted to talk to Adam alone, and she wanted out of the middle of whatever had just happened between Amalia and Steffy. She could explain herself to Amy later, after she knew what Adam was up to. After a minute, he appeared in the hallway behind her, frowning. Satisfied, she took off down another long hallway she hadn't explored yet. Through the second open door on the right, she spotted a large dim library and darted inside. Adam followed her.

Chapter Seven

Sadie shut the door behind them, furtively glancing about the cozy library to make sure they were alone. She turned to Adam, who was still standing by the door, face carefully blank.

"Okay, spill it."

His jaw tightened and his gaze flickered around the room. Focusing on anything but her.

"Adam Michael Stroop—"

He held up a hand to stop her, gesturing to keep it down. She raised an eyebrow. She wasn't going to let this go. When he was still silent, she crossed her arms over her chest and leaned back against a high-back chair.

"You're not supposed to be here," he said finally, his voice a scandalized whisper. "You're not on the guest list."

"Well the mountain decided to cut off the road, almost killing us both, so here I am."

"Had I known you were going to be here, I wouldn't have come." She drew in a quick breath and his cheeks reddened. "I don't mean it that way. It's just—it's dangerous for you to know who I really am."

"So you admit you're putting on some sort of farce? The camera crew, the documentary? The fake name?"

He winced, glancing about the library once more. Did he think the place was bugged? Someone was hiding behind the curtains? Listening through a peephole behind the portrait of a mutton-chopped cowboy above the fireplace?

"I..." he stalked towards her, grabbing her arm and pulling her to the window. He sat on the window seat bench and pulled her down with him. He leaned in close. He smelled like after-shave, leather, and books. Or maybe the book smell was coming from the library. "You need to play along. Here, I'm Nick Walker. I'm a documentarian that's following the company owners to do a fluff piece on how great they are. And that's all you need to know."

Sadie scoffed. Fat chance of that. She was opening her mouth to speak her mind when they heard voices outside the door.

"Did you lock that?" Adam asked, panic tinging his voice.

"Um...no?"

"Shit." He looked around, then pulled the curtain to close off the window seat. "Put your feet up," he hissed.

Seriously?

The door was opening now. Adam pulled his feet up and Sadie did the same, her mind whirling. What was he involved in? What were all of them involved in, now that they were all stuck together? Crowded together on the bench seat, side by side, barely breathing, Sadie couldn't believe her luck. First, she got stuck here after almost dying. Then, she ran into an old friend...flame?...pretending to be someone they weren't. And now...she was hiding in a library, behind a dusty curtain. Her nose tickled.

Footsteps on the carpet moved closer. Her eyes flicked to

Adam's. How would they explain themselves if they were caught?

Why were they hiding, anyway?

A second set of footsteps entered. Then they heard low voices from near the fireplace.

"This is bullshit," a male voice said lowly, his voice just short of furious.

"Bad luck," a female voice said, placatingly.

"Too much bad luck piling up," the man said.

"You think I somehow made the mountain fall?"

A scoff, and then something that sounded more...amorous.

Sadie tried to place the voices, but she didn't know anyone here well enough to guess who was now embracing in the library. Was this an illicit liaison? Or was this just one of the many couples here? Rosalie and Freddy? She hadn't seen them so much as look at each other tonight. Amalia and Jonathan? The quiet Bautistas? Brent and Kenna? What about Steffy and Jon Jr? They certainly seemed close.

A log in the fireplace popped, and it must have startled the couple apart, because they were talking again.

"Without the Joneses here, I don't think we can make our move."

"We don't need them. We have the McCoy sisters. They're bleeding money and followers after that disastrous live sale."

"Idiots. To say that kind of shit when they were live..."

The conversation got low then, and Sadie couldn't make out all the words. Her nose was getting itchier. She glanced at Adam, who was still listening intently. Her eyes watered. She poked him, and he snapped his gaze to her, eyes widening when he realized she was holding in a sneeze. He shook his head madly.

Sadie clamped a hand over her mouth and nose, hoping she

could contain it. Ms. Beatrice must not get to these curtains often, it was the first thing in the house that wasn't pristine.

"I need to go back before I'm missed," the woman said. Hmm...so perhaps not one of the established couples. *Scandalous.*

The man grumbled, but he must have assented, because they heard soft footfalls on the carpet, and then the door closed. Had they both left? Sadie hoped so, because she wasn't going to hold the sneeze in much longer.

Just as it burst forth, Sadie heard the sound of books being shuffled. It stopped abruptly. Adam held his breath, shifting forward as if to bolt through the curtain to protect her if needed.

But then the door shut.

They lingered in the quiet. Had the person actually left? Or were they just trying to flush them out?

Finally, Adam peeked around the edge of the curtain. He relaxed. "There's no one there."

"Thank God," Sadie grumbled, climbing off of the bench. Her knees screamed from being in the same position for so long, her sore ankle from her outdoor escapades pounding. She stomped over to the desk and grabbed a tissue, blowing her nose noisily.

"We have to get out of here," Adam said then. "If he heard us, he's going to be looking to see who's not at the main gathering."

"Who was that?"

Adam looked grim. "I'm not sure."

"Really? What were they talking about? Some sort of deal? Is that why you're doing this cloak and dagger thing?"

"Seriously, Sadie. You've always been nosy, but this is a new commitment."

Sadie rolled her eyes. "You have no idea. Someone spray

painted one of my coffee kiosks with the words 'Nosy Bitch' a few months ago. I've decided to lean into it."

He quirked a smile. "You're the same as always."

"You aren't."

"It's been a long time." The smile was gone.

"Let me help you. I'm pretty good at unraveling mysteries."

"No."

Sadie felt frustration building up in her. She was stuck on this mountain with a group in which she most definitely did not belong with absolutely nothing to do. She wanted in on the sleuthing. But then she looked at Adam closely, noticing for the first time the stress in the set of his jaw, the clench of his fists, the worry lines on his forehead. Adam had always been intense. A man that carried a lot of responsibility and felt the weight of it always. If he was being this insistent with her...maybe Sadie didn't want to know. This wasn't a lark. This was serious. She was going to be here just until she could get out, and then she was flouncing from the situation. The least she could do was not make it harder on him.

She sighed. "Okay."

"Why don't I believe you?"

"Because you've always been a smart man. But it's okay. I'm supposed to be on vacation. I'm going to see if they have any tequila at that bar, take a shot, and further stuff myself with some of those canapés before toddling off to bed. I'm in the Rockchuck suite if you decide you need my help."

And with that, Sadie swept out the door.

* * *

She walked in the room to squeals of delight.

Amalia, Rosalie, and Glenn stood around a large cardboard box, and the gathered retailers were descending on it, shrieking.

50

Even the men were involved, shouldering each other out of the way to get first dibs. The Valentines watched, their smiles both calculated and delighted as they watched the chaos their product was causing.

It quickly turned vicious.

Amy came out of the middle of the growing dog pile triumphant, her arms full of plastic-wrapped packages of brightly colored clothing. "I got the roses!" She shouted, grinning at Sadie. She didn't see Steffy behind her, the short woman getting up on her tiptoes to snatch the rose-printed leggings from Amy's hands.

"I had them first," Steffy shouted.

Amy's face fell, the look she gave Steffy murderous. She glanced back at Sadie, tossing the rest of her armful at her before turning to chase Steffy down. Sadie caught most of what Amy threw, a few pieces bouncing onto the floor only to be quickly snatched up by Kenna, who eyed Sadie like she was going to try to take away what she had. Sadie growled at her, and she scurried off.

"You bitch!" Steffy screamed, and Sadie saw Amy marching away from her determinedly, the leggings clutched over her chest. The film crew followed her every move, obviously having caught their full exchange. Sadie wondered how that would be depicted in a puff piece about Glamarosa, but Amy was in front of her then, grabbing what Sadie was holding and telling her she was going to run it up to her room and then be back. She was gone before Sadie could ask what the hell had even just happened.

The empty box was whisked away, and the sellers disappeared from the room, presumably to lock up their goods. The Valentines laughed amongst themselves at the chaos they'd created, and Sadie took advantage of the cleared out room to find a bottle of tequila, discreetly take a shot, and then fill her plate at the dwindling buffet—her desserts were already gone, she noted with pride. She took her plate and another glass of wine to a dark corner of the room and settled in to do some people watching. The soft bed upstairs was calling her name, but she needed to think through her day first.

People reentered, and the groups in the room settled, people sitting, talking. Amy sat next to the Bautistas, their heads together as they talked earnestly. Sadie still hadn't changed like she'd promised Amy she would, so she was glad it seemed she hadn't spotted her. Glenn held court with Steffy, who kept looking at Amy darkly, and the McCoy sisters. Amalia and Rosalie were laughing with Kenna while their husbands drank Scotch at the bar, grumbling at one another. Amalia kept sending glares in Steffy's direction. Jon Jr was scrolling his phone in the corner, though he seemed to watch Steffy more than do anything on his phone. Titus and the lawyer had disappeared, perhaps already heading up to bed. It was almost ten o'clock.

Amalia gathered the girls around to ogle a set of plans she unrolled on a table.

"The house that Glamarosa built!" She exclaimed as everyone oohed and awwed. Sadie didn't join them, her stomach twisting from the tequila and the mention of "twelve bathrooms!" and "an Olympic-size swimming pool" and "floor to ceiling Italian marble". Apparently, Glamarosa was doing great. Sadie wondered if their Glamaristas were doing as well.

Sadie yawned.

The itinerary left in her room said the morning started at seven with yoga, followed by a breakfast buffet, and the first work session at nine. Sadie planned to skip the yoga and the work session, but not the breakfast. Her e-reader was full of smutty books and mysteries she'd been saving for her trip and staying cuddled up in that amazing bed with it sounded like the perfect way to spend a day stuck on a mountain, the possibility of the chalet sweeping away in another landslide at any moment always at the back of her mind.

Someone moved in the corner of her eye and she realized the documentary crew had already faded into the background for her. She wondered if its subjects even paid attention to them anymore. What could they be capturing that they might not like?

And what was Adam's game? Whatever he was up to, he was taking it very seriously. The last time Sadie had talked to him was several years ago, when he'd been busy at a startup. Something to do with wearable technology. Tracking sleep patterns? She couldn't quite remember. Why would he be posing as someone he wasn't? Were the videographer and boom mic guy also in on it?

And who had been talking in the library? What were they planning? How had the landslide changed their plans? And what had the McCoys said on their live sale that had their business crumbling? What did that have to do with making a move?

Sadie tipped her wineglass to finish the last drops and sighed. She was tired from the trauma of the day. Her full belly, the alcohol, and the warm fire wasn't helping. She wasn't going to solve any mystery tonight—if there was one afoot, anyway—so she might as well head up to bed. And she'd told Adam she wouldn't get involved.

The hallways were dim and deserted when Sadie slipped upstairs after waving at Amy as she left the great room. She felt pulled to the kitchen to help Gavin clean up, but her feet forced her towards her room, where a giant box, similar to the one that had just been ravaged downstairs, blocked the door. Sadie hadn't expected Glamarosa to be so generous. What they'd given her was surely more than she could fit in a whole other suitcase. She hoped it wasn't a box of as sought after stuff as what had been downstairs. She didn't want to end up like Cinderella, standing in tatters after her evil stepsisters ripped the clothes off of her.

She opened her door with the key Ms. Beatrice had slipped her at the beginning of dinner, then pushed the box into the room just far enough she could close the door behind her and lock it. She should probably go through what they'd picked out for her, hang up a couple of things so it wasn't all wrinkled. But the luxurious bed was calling her.

Fuck it, I'm on vacation. Sadie sped through her bedtime routine, falling into bed as soon as she could. When she turned out the light, she checked her phone. 11:06 p.m.

Chapter Eight

Loud voices outside her room woke her up.

Sadie sat up straight, her heart pounding. Was the mountain sliding again?

She perked her ears for the rumblings she would hear in her nightmares for years to come, for the ground to quake beneath her, but the earth was still and quiet.

It was only the humans in the chalet yelling.

She reached for her phone on the bedside table. It was 1:02 a.m.

"I know it was you!" This voice was shrill, feminine, a contrast from the manly shouts of moments ago. Was that Amy? *Shit.*

Sadie sprung from her bed, remembering to grab her glasses at the last moment, the world around her coming into dim focus as she hurried to her door, tripping over the box of clothing as she did.

She could only see figures through the peephole, no faces, so she stood next to the door, heart beating rapidly, ear pressed against it, to try to make out what was being said, to try to identify the voices. If Amy was out there, Sadie would get involved.

Otherwise, she would stay in her room. *Stay in your room*, she repeated to herself. *Nothing happening in this chalet is your business.*

"You lie!" Another woman's voice, accusatory.

"Calm down," a man's voice, with authority. Sadie winced. What an unhelpful de-escalation tactic.

"She's out to get me!"

Sadie couldn't distinguish the voices. She needed to see if Amy as involved. She opened her door a crack.

The scene in the hallway defied reason. Kenna and Steffy were being kept apart by a harried Glenn. The perfectly coiffed, composed women of earlier had devolved into makeup-smeared, ratty haired banshees, shrieking curses at each other. Brett was on the ground, hand over his eye, blood trickling from his nose. Alex held a camera, filming the entire scene, Adam behind him with an inscrutable look on his face holding a boom mic. Had she stumbled onto some sort of Bad Girls Club reality TV set? Why were two of the top Glamarosa sellers trying to fight outside her room in the middle of the night? Who had decked Brett?

No one noticed her ogling.

"This is not the Glamarosa way," Glenn said, his voice stern. "We are all one family. We bring opportunity and substance to lives. We do not fight with one another, physically or otherwise."

Steffy rolled her eyes but stopped grappling with Glenn, composing herself and slinking back to lean against the wall. "I didn't do anything to her. She started it."

"She's such a liar!" Kenna screeched again. Brett rose to his feet wearily. Kenna gestured at him. "She punched Brett!"

Sadie stifled a grunt of surprise. Tiny Steffy Austin had done that damage to Ken? Yikes.

"Because he put his hands on me!"

"Because you were stealing something from our room!"

"I got lost," Steffy said, shrugging. "I forgot what room was mine."

Kenna's face turned red, and she lunged for Steffy again, but Brett caught her. "Enough," he said lowly, in her ear.

"It is enough, McKenna." Glenn's use of Kenna's real name seemed to snap her out of it. "I believe Steffy. Remember to come from a place of trust."

"I don't trust her," Kenna said, but she let Brett pull her down the hallway. "And you shouldn't either, Glenn. Why not trust *me*, instead? She was stealing from us, Glenn!"

Steffy huffed but didn't engage.

"I'll escort you to your actual room, Steffy," Glenn said, offering his arm to her. "We'll talk about this later, Brett," he added over his shoulder. That he addressed that at Brett instead of Kenna put Sadie's back up. Big control your wife vibes. Yuck. As they moved past Sadie's room, Steffy's eyes caught hers, and Sadie thought she saw victory there. The film crew came by next, following them up the hallway towards wherever Steffy's room was, and Sadie caught Adam's eye.

"See?" He mouthed to her.

She shrugged and closed the door.

So Glamarosa might not be entirely the happy family they liked to pretend they were. That still didn't explain Adam's deceit, his worry, his paranoia.

What Sadie knew, was that none of it was her business. And while she could be a nosy bitch when she needed or wanted to be, she was going to stay out of this one. Adam could have his fun. She was going back to bed.

But the next time Sadie was awoken, it was by a quiet knock on the door.

Outside was Adam, his face ashen.

"I need your help," he whispered.

And just like that, it became her problem.

* * *

Sadie hustled him inside, locking the door behind him. She steered him around the Glamarosa box, then to the chair next to the window, where he collapsed.

She bolted into the bathroom for a glass of water, then came back to hand it to him. She sat on the bed, facing him, and waited while he took a drink.

His hands shook.

"I–" he stopped, gulped down more water. Took a deep breath. "Steffy Austin is dead."

"What?" Sadie shrieked. That was impossible. She'd just seen her, hours ago. What time was it, anyway? It was dark out, snow still falling heavily.

"Jeez, be quiet," Adam reprimanded, wincing and looking at the door.

Sadie's mind whirled.

"You can't just come in here and drop that kind of news and expect me to be quiet about it!"

"You said you'd help me!"

His initial words penetrated, finally, and she felt a tendril of fear wind up her back. "Why...would you need help?" She glanced around the room. She had nothing she could use as a weapon. But...surely he wasn't dangerous, right? What Sadie remembered most of Adam from grad school was his singular commitment to raising his younger sister after their parent's deaths, who was still in high school at the time. Surely a man like that wasn't a man that could be violent. Right?

"I didn't do anything to her! I just...found her. Just now."

"Did you call the police?"

"No. No. I guess I need to."

"Trust me, I've done this once or twice before. First step is to call the police."

Adam stared at her with confusion, but she waved it off. There'd be time to explain *that* later.

"Get out your cell phone. Call now."

"I...I don't think I should. I'm using a false name!"

Sadie groaned. "What are you involved in, Adam? I'm not getting in the middle."

"You wanted in last night in the library. Hiding behind the curtain and eavesdropping!"

Sadie buried her head in her hands. *This was not happening again.* She wasn't even supposed to be here. And, shit. Poor Steffy Austin. A thought occurred to her.

"Wait, you're sure she's dead?" Sadie hopped up. "Did you try to revive her? What happened, anyway?"

Adam got paler, which Sadie wouldn't have said was possible even a minute ago.

"Adam?"

"She's...she's definitely dead." He put a shaky hand to his mouth. Sadie sighed. Everything about this was a bad idea.

"Fine, I'll call."

She grabbed her phone from the nightstand, swiped it open, the screen declaring it 4:07 a.m. She opened her dialer...and stopped.

"Shit."

"What?"

"There's no service. Wi-Fi or cell. I can't call out."

Adam pulled his phone out of his pocket and checked the screen. "Oh damn."

"We have to tell Ms. Beatrice, then. She has a sat phone."

"Okay. Okay. She stays in the guesthouse above the garage. We can do that." He stood.

"You can do that. I'm staying here."

Adam frowned at her. "There could be a killer roaming the halls, and you're sending me out alone?"

"She was *murdered*?" Sadie pushed him, and he sat back down at the force before popping back up. "I thought you meant she'd fallen down the stairs or something!"

"No." He shook his head violently. "It was on purpose. Very obviously. She's in her room."

"What were you doing in her room?"

"I wasn't. Her room is across from mine. I heard a loud noise. I opened my door and saw her door was ajar. I called her name, then pushed the door open when she didn't answer, and... I saw her." He gulped hard, his handsome face anguished.

"Oh, Adam." Sadie wrapped her arms around him. "I'm sorry. I'll go with you. Of course I will. I'll watch your back."

They took a moment to compose themselves. Adam splashed his face with water in the bathroom. Sadie pulled leggings on under her oversized sleep t-shirt and layered a cardigan over the top. There was a chill in the air, and not just from the unseasonably cold weather. Something bad had happened in the chalet tonight.

But as they opened the door and started into the hallway, a scream broke the heavy silence.

They were too late.

Chapter Nine

They rushed toward the scream, down the hall, around the corner, and came to a stop. Outside Steffy's open door, white faced, curlers in her hair, was Shayna McCoy, the older of the sisters. In front of their eyes, she fainted to the floor.

The hallway filled with people then, and the next few minutes were a blur. Ms. Beatrice appeared, then rushed off to call the police. Shayna was revived and ushered down the hall by her sister. Leo Bautista was called for, rushed in, then came back out quickly, grim-faced. Adam's crew showed up, and Glenn, and then Glenn and Adam started arguing if it was appropriate for the crew to be filming. Amy wandered down the stairs, sleep in her eyes, and stumbled to the door. It was then Sadie rushed forward, finally. Amy's face crumpled, and Sadie reached her right as she began to collapse. She held her in her arms as she sagged.

"That's...impossible," she said. "I just saw her!"

"I know, I know," Sadie assured her. She tried to move her away from the door, but Amy was a dead weight. "Let's move, you don't need to see this."

"But those are my leggings," Amy whispered then, and Sadie snapped her head to look at her, realizing, for the first time, that Amy wasn't as out of it as she appeared. And what did she mean, her leggings? Sadie had resolutely kept her eyes off whatever was causing women to faint and men to emerge pale and grim, but something in Amy's eyes made her realize she needed to look. Bracing herself, reminding herself it wasn't the first dead body she'd ever seen, Sadie looked into the room.

Her own knees went weak.

Inside, Steffy Austin lay on her bed. The bedside table lamp cast melodramatic shadows over the room, but illuminated her still, twisted, lifeless face. Wrapped around her neck, fashioned in a grotesque bow, was a familiar pair of leggings—black with red roses, the limited edition ones Steffy and Amy had fought over last night. Her rose necklace sat in the middle of the bow, a gruesome decoration.

"Everyone out of the hallway," Glenn boomed behind them. "Everyone go into the great room now and wait there!"

Sadie didn't want to do that. She wanted to go back to her room, lock the door behind her, bury herself under the covers, and force herself to forget what she'd just seen. She wanted to bring Amy with her, keep her safe, too.

But she allowed her and Amy to be swept down the hallway, down the stairs, picking up confused people who hadn't rushed towards the screams as they went, until they were all herded into the great room. It was cold, and dim, and Amy and Sadie huddled together on their usual couch, a blanket thrown over them. Leo made a fire in the fireplace. Everyone stood or sat together with quiet, ashen faces.

The film crew had stayed behind in the hallway, still arguing with Glenn. Sadie had snuck a glance at Adam as she left, but he hadn't looked at her.

What would happen to them now?

Who had done this awful thing?

Sadie looked around the room again. They were stuck in this chalet, with no way in or out. Whoever had done this to Steffy was probably in this room with them, right this moment. Had it been a random act? Or a crime perpetuated against Steffy specifically? A chill racked her, and she pulled the blanket up over her arms. Either way, they could all be in danger. As witnesses.

Amalia and Rosalie sat across from them, sobbing, each being comforted by their husbands. Jon Jr's face was racked with grief, though he was dry-eyed. He sat on the arm of the couch, staring off into the distance. What had his and Steffy's connection really been? A casual hookup? Love?

Brett and Kenna stood by the now-glowing fireplace, and in the dark shadows of the room, Sadie could see a blossoming bruise under his right eye, one Kenna insisted Steffy had given him.

Titus, the aloof designer, stood staring out the window at the cold, dark, snowy morning. Sadie narrowed her eyes at him. No, he was staring at his reflection in the window, she corrected herself as he plucked an errant eyebrow hair before perusing himself again. He didn't seem very broken up.

Paul, the lawyer, was wearing flannel pajamas and fuzzy slippers, his curly hair standing straight up as he wandered around the room with his phone, apparently trying to get a signal. As head legal counsel for Glamarosa, he had to be thinking about the repercussions for the company.

Lexi was curled into her husband's side, head buried in his armpit as her body racked with sobs. Sadie had never seen her and Steffy exchange two words, but the impression Sadie had gotten of her was that she was a sweet, sensitive woman. Of course she'd be broken up about this.

Which brought her to the McCoy sisters.

Who were decidedly *not* broken up about the death of one of their fellow Glamaristas.

Shayna had recovered from her faint and was playing a game on her phone, which was not on silent, and the sounds of successful match threes and coins accumulating mingled with the snapping of the logs in the fireplace and the sobs around the room. She looked bored. Julie appeared to be asleep, her pink satin eye mask pulled down as she lounged on a chaise.

Beside Sadie, Amy was sniffling. Her eyes were red, the bags under them making it apparent she hadn't slept well last night, even before her rude awakening. Again, Sadie felt that tendril of something not being right go through her. Nothing about this had been right from the moment she'd pulled up to the chalet. As soon as she could, she was getting Amy alone so she could ask her some questions.

Ms. Beatrice and Gavin coming into the room stopped that line of thought.

Ms. Beatrice looked grim, and Gavin looked bewildered. He looked different out of his chef's coat, wearing a t-shirt that stretched across his shoulders and showed off his tattooed forearms and a pair of sweatpants. His hair was mussed, and he wore glasses. He'd obviously just been awoken.

"Where's Mr. Valentine, and the film crew?" Ms. Beatrice asked shrilly after taking in the absences in the room.

"My uncle is staked out at Steffy's door," Jon Jr said, his voice breaking as he spoke her name, the first words he'd spoken that morning. "And the film crew's watching him."

Ms. Beatrice huffed. "Right. Gavin, you watch this group and make sure no one leaves. I'm going to secure Steffy's room, and I'll return with everyone. Then I'm supposed to call the sheriff back."

"What do you mean watch this group?" Freddy Bianchi, Rosalie's husband, said, standing. His tone was belligerent, but he was speaking to Ms. Beatrice's straight back as she walked away from him.

Gavin held up his hands. "I've been deputized by Ms. B, and I've only been up ten minutes. Be gentle."

Jonathan, Amalia's husband, sniffed. "None of us would have done this to that poor girl."

"We're the only ones here," Sadie blurted, immediately regretting her outburst. All eyes in the room snapped to hers, even Julie's, who lifted her eye mask. Sadie shrugged, her cheeks burning under the scrutiny. "No one can get in or out, right? So...it was one of us."

Lexi moaned, Leo rubbing her back and speaking comforting words.

Amalia let out a loud sob.

"She could have done something to herself," Kenna said. At the outraged cries that rose from the room, she shrugged.

"I don't believe she could've done...what was done...to herself," Leo said in a gritty voice.

"Leo is right. And this young lady is right," a voice said from the door, and all eyes in the room shifted from Sadie to the entrance of Glenn, who had spoken, followed by the film crew and Ms. Beatrice. "Someone killed our friend Steffy Austin. And whoever did it is in this room."

* * *

Sadie's heart felt like it might beat out of her chest. She'd been in a room with a killer once before. Well, twice. That she knew of. And both of those times were more outside than inside, but this felt different.

More intimate.

The Wi-Fi was out.

There was no cell phone signal.

Their power was supplied only by a generator, and who knew how long the fuel would last.

The only road in or out had swept away in a landslide.

A late season blizzard had grounded all aircraft that might be able to reach them for rescue.

And there was a killer on the loose.

Amy's hand reached for Sadie's under the blanket, and she gripped it tightly. Sadie had to get them through this. She would get them through this.

Ms. Beatrice addressed them. Glenn had taken a seat between his sisters, their husbands having decamped to the window sitting area to frown at one another. Whatever distance Sadie had seen between the siblings before had vanished in the face of this tragedy. She wondered what they were worried about most—their business, their reputation, the danger they could be in, or Steffy.

"Now, I called the authorities," Ms. Beatrice was saying. "They confirmed they still cannot reach us. I've been instructed to lock Ms. Austin's room, gather everyone together, then call the sheriff so he can address us all."

"What about them?"

Jon Jr's question was accompanied by a chin nod to the camera crew where they'd posted up in the back of the room, where they could see everyone. Adam stood off to the side, looking tense.

"Their contract states they can film anywhere, anytime," Glenn said, annoyed.

"I'll pull my film release," Brett warned. "What happened has nothing to do with Glamarosa–"

"How do you know it doesn't?" Adam interrupted. Brett huffed. "With the authorities not here, I'd think you'd want us to film. No one's going to do anything with the cameras rolling, right?"

Adam had a point, and it seemed to soothe the room as there were no more objections, though she saw Brett whisper in Kenna's ear something that made her smirk.

"If you're quite done," Ms. Beatrice said, "I'll call the sheriff on the sat phone." They listened quietly while she dialed, the long notes of the button pushes loud in the room. A loud ring, and then a male voice picked up on speakerphone.

"Yes, hello?"

"Sheriff, this is Ms. Beatrice from the chalet. 911 told me to call you."

"Of course. You have everyone gathered together?"

"Yes."

"Please, go around the room and introduce yourselves. Ms. Beatrice will take a list of names, residences, and other pertinent information for my records, so don't resist her when she asks." Everyone introduced themselves, Adam not stumbling as he introduced himself as the very fake Nick Walker. Was it a crime to misrepresent yourself to law enforcement in Wyoming? Sadie wasn't sure, but it made her stomach hurt to think about Nick putting himself at risk of suspicion.

"Thank you for your cooperation," the sheriff said when he was done. "My name is Wilson Wise. I'm the sheriff of Teton County. First, I want to apologize that you're all still stuck there. Ms. Beatrice has told me that while you still have power, your Wi-Fi connection has gone out, and as usual, there is no cell coverage. I understand that could be alarming. Please know that though you cannot call out, we have not forgotten about you, and we are mounting a full-scale rescue as soon as we can get to you. Unfortunately, this storm is set to continue for at least another twenty-four hours, and our resources are stretched thin with people in trouble across the county. This storm came out of. nowhere and surprised us all."

There were disappointed groans.

"I know, I know. Spring in the Tetons. Sadie can tell you all about it." Sadie jolted at the call out to her, specifically. She knew Sheriff Wise, of course. She hadn't voted for him in the last election, preferring his younger, more progressive opponent, but he'd always been kind to her. When the Jackson Police Department had initiated their informal boycott of her bakery after she put a Black Lives Matter sticker on the door, Sheriff Wise had still come in for his regular order—a large black coffee and a slice of the vegetarian quiche of the day. She'd never worked closely with him, like she had with the lead detective of the Jackson Police Department, Will Nolan, but she guessed she shouldn't be surprised that he would know her history with investigating. She wondered if his mentioning her was an informal warning to keep her nose out of this. She wondered if she would heed his warning.

Sheriff Wise was still talking.

"—as soon as the weather clears, we'll have a helicopter headed up to begin evacuating you. Now, on to the reason we're having this discussion." He cleared his throat, and Sadie could picture his face on the other end of the line. Grave, with his salt and pepper mustache quivering as he thought how to put his words. "I understand there has been a suspicious death."

"Sheriff," Leo said. "If you don't mind, I'm Dr. Leo Bautista, an emergency department doctor from Las Vegas. I examined the victim, and I feel confident saying it's more than suspicious. She was murdered."

The sheriff was quiet for a moment. "Thank you for your professional opinion, Dr. Bautista. Well—you see, we have a quandary. You all are fine, upstanding citizens, and you're stuck up there. And one of you is dead, perhaps killed. And I can't reach you to keep you safe. So, I need to ask you all a favor. You need to keep each other safe. Ms. Beatrice has locked the victim's room, and it's off limits by my order. You need to stay in pairs, and never be alone. The bigger the group you can be in, the better. Lock your doors when you're in your rooms. Don't let anyone in."

He let that sink in.

"Here at the sheriff's office, our job is to seek truth. We owe it to Ms. Austin to find out the truth behind this matter, so I'm going to ask you to not speculate. Do not investigate. Keep to yourselves, and just hang tight until we can get to you. I understand you have plenty of provisions. I would expect we can reach you tomorrow morning, if the forecast I've seen holds."

Another night of this. A night stuck with these people, with undercurrents she didn't understand, with a murderer on the loose. She'd so much rather be in Cabo. Or really, anywhere but here.

"One last thing. Since this incident is clear in your minds now, I'm going to ask you each to write out a statement this morning, right now, before you do anything else, starting with your travel to the chalet and up until this minute. Include everything. My detectives and I will go over them with you after we get you out. And—if your Wi-Fi comes up or you suddenly get a signal, hear me now. This news stays quiet until it's released by the sheriff's office. No one is allowed to tell anyone outside the chalet what has happened. If anyone does, if Ms. Austin's loved ones find out about this from the news instead of through proper channels...you will suffer legal consequences. Understood?"

They all said they did, and Sadie looked at everyone in turn. The Bautistas and Valentines were solemn. The McCoys were petulant. Brett and Kenna were angry. Jon Jr had his head in his hands. Amy, next to her, looked frightened. "Now, I'd like you all to get started on your statements. I'm sure Ms. Beatrice can find everyone paper and pens. Before I go, know that I will check in with Ms. Beatrice at noon today, and again at six. If anything comes up between now and then, Ms. Beatrice is to call me immediately."

They all said their okays, but before the sheriff hung up, he said, "now, Ms. B, if you can hand the phone to Sadie Moose, please."

Everyone in the room went silent. And they were all looking at her.

Chapter Ten

Dawn light was blooming outside when Sadie took the satellite phone into the library, closing and locking the door behind her as directed by Sheriff Wise. She'd taken him off speaker phone, also as he'd directed, then found a place they could talk alone. Sadie could only imagine this made her look suspicious. And what had happened to never being alone? She glanced around the dim library. She eyed the painting of the mutton-chopped cowboy over the fireplace. Well, she was alone except for Mr. Chops.

She walked to the window seat where her and Adam had hidden the night before and put the phone back up to her ear.

"Sheriff? I'm alone now."

"And you locked the door behind you?"

"Yes. I thought you said to never be alone?"

"After this, I don't want you to be, but I wanted a private word with you."

"Okay..."

"Sadie, Will Nolan is a good friend of mine."

"Of course he is."

"Jackson's a small town. Even if I didn't know what you'd

been up to in past investigations from him, I'd know it, anyway. I need to tell you something, and I need you to listen carefully."

Sadie knew what was coming. *Stay out of my investigation.* She could almost hear him saying it. She was so sure of it, when he spoke his next words, she had to ask him to repeat himself.

"I said, I need your help."

Sadie gulped. "What? Me?"

"Yes, you. I know you have a keen mind and a way of getting people to talk. I can't be there to solve this murder, and I need you to be my eyes and ears. Can you do that for me? Listen to conversations. Take notes. These first few hours after a crime has been committed are key to solving the case, and I can't be there to do it. I know I can trust you."

"How do you know I didn't kill her?"

"If you didn't kill Sloan Brackenridge, then I know you wouldn't kill anybody, no matter how mad they made you."

He had a point. Sadie hadn't killed her lifelong nemesis, Sloan Brackenridge, but she'd been the number one suspect in the crime after being in a very public argument with her the day of her murder and her body was found—by Sadie!—in the alley behind her house. She'd also been killed with a pie server with Sadie's name on it. That Sadie hadn't actually done that...was a pretty good vote of confidence that she wasn't the murdering type.

"And I've owed you a debt of gratitude for solving Royce Hensley's murder, too. You know Royce was one my reserve deputies. He was a real asshole, but he was still my friend." Royce, the body she and Jake found in the hot springs pool during a romantic interlude. Sadie shuddered.

"You're...welcome?" This really wasn't going the way Sadie thought it would go.

"And I need your help here. Can I count on you? Let me give you my direct line, just in case you get a signal and can call or text me." He rattled off a number, and Sadie inputted it into her cell phone. "Now tell me about the crime scene. Have you seen it?"

Sadie thought hard about what she'd seen in Steffy's room and relayed the details. Steffy had been lying on her back in her bed. She'd been wearing a pair of loose gray pants and a t-shirt with the Glamarosa logo on it. Her legs had been straight, arms crossed across her chest. *Staged*, was the word that came to Sadie's mind. It looked like the scene had been staged. She described the grotesque bow, the pattern of the leggings, the necklace placed on top of the bow. Her face. Her poor, poor face.

When she was done, Sheriff Wise asked a series of questions.

No, she hadn't noticed signs of a struggle.

No, she hadn't seen any blood.

No, she hadn't seen anything else unusual in the room. Aside from the dead body.

Sadie left out the part about Adam finding Steffy's body first for now. After all, he'd only asked about the crime scene, and Sadie wanted to know more about what Adam was up to before she told that part.

"Everyone's going to ask me what you wanted to talk to me about," she said when he was done grilling her. She didn't want to think that she might have a target on her back now.

"Tell them it was about bakery business. Some sort of legal thing I'm investigating for you that I needed to give you an update on." That wasn't a terrible idea.

"Okay."

"I'll be checking in again at noon. Give the phone back to Ms. Beatrice, but I'll let her know I want to talk to you at some point this afternoon and she can sneak you the phone. Do you have somebody to buddy up with?"

"My friend Amy. The reason I'm stuck here." *The person whose leggings were wrapped around Steffy's neck.* But she didn't say that part out loud. Amy hadn't killed Steffy. There was no way.

"Okay. Stick close together, and we'll talk soon. Thank you."

He hung up, and Sadie dropped the boxy phone onto the window seat. She laid her forehead against the cool glass and took a deep breath. Her intuition had said, as soon as she'd gotten here, that something was amiss at the chalet. From Amy's behavior to the landslide to the vibes at last night's dinner to the secret library conversation and the film crew to the weird rush on clothes to the fight in the hall last night, she'd wanted to know what was going on. Now, she'd been directed by the sheriff to help find a murderer.

Well, she guessed she had a reputation to uphold.

And, it would be something to do.

"Just call me Sadie Moose, Lady Detective," she declared in the quiet of the room. But here she didn't have her loyal sidekicks to help her. No Kendall, or the knowledge she gleaned from everyone she met with contacts everywhere. No Kamari, who could smell bullshit from a mile away. No Penny, who worked at the newspaper and always knew the town scoop. No Mateo, her best friend Paige's husband and also her lawyer, who could tell her when she was being too trusting of law enforcement. And no Tyrone, her soft-eared moose-eyed dog who brought her peace, solace, and comfort.

No, here she had a loyal if distant friend who was in this business up to her eyeballs, a kind of ex-flame that was using an alias, and a celebrity chef who seemed to know more than he said he did. She took another deep breath, then squared her shoulders. Steffy Austin deserved justice. If Sadie could help her get it and make sure her friends escaped suspicion and stayed safe in the process? She would do it. She would always do it.

* * *

All eyes were on Sadie as she walked back into the great room. She handed the phone to Ms. Beatrice, who was watching her curiously, then sat back down next to Amy. Everyone had yellow notepads and pens and were making their way through their statements.

"What was that about?" Amy whispered.

"I'll tell you later," Sadie said, then picked up her own notepad. What was she supposed to write? The truth? Her eyes flitted to Adam, who was watching her intently. Ms. Beatrice interrupted before she could make a decision.

"Chef Gavin will have breakfast for everyone in the dining room at seven. I take it yoga is canceled, correct?"

"Steffy was leading the session," Glenn said soberly, his voice wavering. "It's canceled." Kenna and the McCoy sisters pouted. "But we'll meet for general session as planned. The sheriff said we should stick together. Might as well continue with our plan. Steffy would want us to continue to learn from one another. She loved Glamarosa."

Blargh. Sadie didn't want to sit through a general session of Glamarosa bullshit. Maybe she could go hang with Gavin instead.

Sighing, Sadie looked down at her notepad. Start with her travel. Fine. She could do that. She would tell the truth. By the time the sheriff collected these statements, it wouldn't matter that Adam was using a false name, wouldn't matter that Adam found Steffy's body first. Because Sadie would have already found the killer.

Chapter Eleven

Since Amy was traveling alone, Sadie was, naturally, her buddy.

After they turned in their statements to Ms. Beatrice, who put them in a manila envelope without looking at them, everyone returned to their rooms. Sadie and Amy had walked quickly past Steffy's room, which was not only locked, but had a handmade sign marked "DO NOT ENTER BY ORDER OF THE TETON COUNTY SHERIFF" written on it in Sharpie. Amy shuddered as they walked by.

First, they stopped in Sadie's room. Amy plopped down on Sadie's bed as Sadie entered the bathroom to gather things to get ready in Amy's suite.

"I can't believe this happened," she moaned.

"It's wild, for sure," Sadie commiserated from the bathroom.

"Steffy was always such a vibrant, bubbly person. I can't imagine who'd want to do this to her."

"And with your leggings."

"They probably weren't mine. I was overreacting. There's more than one pair of those in the world."

"Well, it was someone here. Tell me more about Steffy. She's from California?"

"No, somewhere near Seattle. She's single, no kids. Used to work in fashion merchandising before she started selling Glamarosa. She's a little hip, a little glam, a little punk rock."

Right. Her rainbow hair, her heavy eye makeup, her slightly more hip styling of the flashy clothing.

"And a big seller."

"She has over 30,000 people in her Facebook group where she does most of her sales. I haven't heard her specify exact numbers, but she was in the top ten sellers last year, so she must have sold in the seven to eight figures."

"Jeez, Amy. You're not selling that much...are you?" Sadie exited the bathroom with a bag of toiletries.

Amy was lying on the bed, staring up at the ceiling. "No. Not seven figures, but I moved over $350,000 in product last year. I'm in the top fifty sellers."

"But that's not all profit, right?"

Amy sat up and groaned. "No. About forty percent or so is profit, but I just have to keep buying more and more and more."

"Are you still turning a profit, then?"

"I need to run the numbers this quarter. It's gotten harder to sell. When I first started, this stuff...it just sold itself, seriously. But then so many people joined, which is amazing, we need to share the opportunity, but when my top buyers become sellers, I lose my big customers, and they take their friends with them, so it's always a hustle to find new customers. And then the company wants us to convert them to sellers, too."

"And you make money off their sales, right?"

"Right. I get a bonus every time someone signs up under me, and then I get a percentage of their sales. The more people I get, the higher my bonuses."

"So that makes up for the profits slowing down at some point."

"Right. Right. You're right."

Sadie frowned. Amy still wasn't telling her the full story. And if the bigger profit came from building a team, not selling the product...wasn't that the definition of a pyramid scheme? But hey—they basically had all day to figure it out at this point.

"You know if it wasn't going well, if you wanted to pivot to something else...I would help you, right? Of anyone, you can tell me the truth."

"It's going *fine*, Sadie."

Fine. "Okay. Just know I'm here for you either way. Now, help me go through this box of clothes and pick out what you want me to wear today? Style me, Glamarista."

Amy giggled at that, and Sadie was glad to hear it. Her friend was too serious these days. The frown line between her eyebrows was ever present, and she hadn't sung a Broadway tune in the twelve hours they'd been together.

Together, they lugged the box onto the bed and opened it.

Amy screamed.

* * *

Sadie scanned the contents of the box. She didn't see anything worth screaming over. Just a bunch of clothes in plastic bags with a shiny, wildly patterned ring-bound book on top.

"What?" Sadie said as Amy stood, mouth open, eyes wide, staring at the box. "It's not a head, Amy! There's nothing in here worth screaming over, right?"

"The planner," Amy gasped. "That's Steffy's planner!"

Sadie blinked down at the box, then reached in to grab the planner. She flipped it over. On the cover, in embossed gold, was the year, and beneath that, a scripted "A Glamarista's Year Planner".

"How do you know it's hers?"

"Last year the top ten sellers earned custom planners. They announced it at our convention. Steffy picked that pattern, one of the original Glamarosa leggings patterns that everyone was looking for when the company launched. I'd recognize it anywhere!"

"And it wasn't in here last night when you packed the box?"

"I didn't pack the box! I picked clothes out, but Amalia and Rosalie packed the box."

"Why would they put this in here?"

Sadie opened the cover. There, the first page confirmed Amy's assertion. "Property of Steffy Austin" it said in rainbow script.

"I don't know. Where would they have gotten it, anyway? Steffy always had it on her. She carried it in her bag. I saw her with it last night, actually, at dinner! Wasn't this delivered to you while we were at dinner?"

Sadie nodded. "It was here when I came back. Ms. Beatrice dropped it off."

"So where would Ms. Beatrice have gotten her planner?"

"I don't know," Amy said, frowning. "But that thing is full of Steffy's secrets. You should hand it over to the sheriff!"

"What kind of secrets?"

Amy shrugged. "Steffy wasn't well-liked amongst the top sellers. I'm not sure why. I'm not exactly in with that group. This is the first time I've been invited to this kind of intimate event. I just know I've seen rumors, barbs directed at her on Facebook, stuff like that. But the prevailing opinion was that she was shady and kept secrets. A gatekeeper. She always got the best and most product, sold the most product, signed up the most in her downline. How did she do it? How was she so much better than everyone else?"

"Preferential treatment from the Valentines?" Sadie had the book open to the month of April. "According to this, Steffy spent last weekend with Amalia at a spa in Big Sur?"

"What?" Amy snatched the planner from Sadie's hands. "That bitch."

"What was up with her and Jon Jr?"

Amy flipped through pages, frowning. "Everyone said they were having an affair."

"Is Jon Jr married?"

"No?"

"Then why would it be considered an affair?"

"He's the VP of merchandiser relations. In essence, our boss. He shouldn't be sleeping with a retailer."

"So that's probably where the rumors of preferential treatment come from."

"Yeah. Maybe." Amy snapped the book closed, then held it out to Sadie. "You need to keep this safe. It's not fair or ethical for me or any of the other retailers to see it. There's information about her downlines, her prospects, her sales, her plans in there. I feel dirty having seen it already."

Sadie frowned down at the book. Why did she have it? Who had given it to her? And when had they delivered it? If only Sadie had looked in the box last night, she'd know if it had been given to her while Steffy was still alive. Had it just been put in the box by mistake?

"Okay," Sadie agreed. "I'll keep it in my stuff." She slid it in the outside pocket of her suitcase.

"Now, while you pick an outfit for me, explain what you mean by downline. And what in the heck does 'bringing the husbands home' mean?"

Once Sadie got Amy started about the inner workings of the

company, she launched into what Sadie imagined was her speel she gave prospective retailers. She picked out clothes for her, Sadie objecting to a choice only once—"I'm not into pattern mixing, Amy, please!"—and once Sadie had everything gathered up, they left her room and headed upstairs to Amy's room, Amy still prattling about the company.

While Amy got ready, Sadie went over what she'd learned.

"So to sign up as a retailer, you pay for your initial order from Glamarosa. Unlike most multi-level marketing companies, you have to sell your own stock, you don't sell out of a catalog."

"Right." Amy was washing her face with a whirring brush. Sadie made a note to ask her why.

"Initial orders are around eight grand. That's a lot of money."

"Yep. And don't forget we have to buy our own hangers and racks and shipping supplies, etcetera. It adds up."

"Okay. So then you get your boxes of clothes, and you don't know what's inside?"

"You know what sizes and styles you ordered, and you can pick a percentage of prints to solids, but yeah, you don't know *which* limited edition prints or solids you're getting. That's part of the fun!"

"Okay. So you buy at wholesale, and you sell at retail."

"Yep, it's just that simple," Amy chirped. She was using a roller made of...jade?...on her face now. So many steps.

"Except that a portion of your sales go to your upline."

"Right. In exchange for mentorship in the business, a portion of sales go to your upline."

"Automatically?"

"It comes out of our sales. We use the Glamarosa payment system, Rosebud, for all our sales, even cash. Every night, the sales process in the system, and my portion goes to my bank account. Glamarosa pays sales taxes and my fees to my upline."

"So, since you have a downline, every night you get your portion from your downline?"

"No...those come to us as bonus checks from the company."

Sadie frowned. Amy had moved on to makeup and was drawing lines on her face with a highlighter stick. So far, Sadie had washed her face and applied SPF. Next step for her was tinted moisturizer. At this rate, Sadie could be downstairs with her breakfast finished before Amy finished her contouring.

"So how do you keep track of how much your bonuses should be?"

"Ummmmmm, I don't? It comes from Glamarosa."

"How do you know they're paying you the correct amount?"

"Trust."

"Right. That's not something they teach in business school."

Amy shrugged. "It's one of the tenets of the company, of our culture. We need to trust each other, and trust Glamarosa. If we're suspicious of one another, it breeds discontent."

The more Sadie learned about the inner workings Glamarosa, the more almost-cult-like it sounded.

"How much do you get as a bonus when someone signs up?"

"Ten percent of their order."

"So eight hundred dollars?" No wonder Kenna had looked at Sadie like a fresh piece of meat yesterday. She'd been seeing dollar signs above Sadie's head as a potential recruit.

"A lot of people are buying in for more now. It makes sense to start with a big inventory."

"So...you tell them they should buy more? Even though that means you'll have a bigger bonus? Do you...disclose that to them?"

Amy dropped her makeup brush and caught Sadie's eyes in the mirror. "Of course I do."

"Does everyone?"

"I can't control what everyone else does, only myself."

Sadie was silent, thinking about that. Plus, she was putting on eyeliner and mascara, which meant she needed to be silent, staring in the mirror wide-eyed while her mouth was open. Why that face was required when applying mascara, Sadie would never know, she just knew it was universal.

"Are there any downsides to having a downline, besides the fact you lose buyers?"

"Well...it does take up a lot of time to mentor a team. Once you have ten on your team total, so that includes the people in your downline's downlines, you become a silver level rose. Once you have five silvers in your downline, you become gold. Ten golds, you're rose gold. Twenty rose golds, you're platinum. Then it starts into the jewels. I'm currently a gold level, just one silver away from becoming rose gold." Amy gestured at her gold necklace with nine petals, and it suddenly made sense to Sadie. Not the complex system, but the similar-but different rose necklaces all the women of Glamarosa were wearing. That Steffy had been decorated with in death.

Hers had been a silver necklace with several gem petals strung on it, which must mean hers was platinum. Kenna's necklace was rose gold, Lexi's was silver. Maybe platinum, but no jewels, and it hadn't had many petals.

"So you have..." Sadie did the math quickly. "Almost 500 people on your team?"

"Yep."

"That does take a lot of time, then."

"I have a Facebook group for my team. I have to make sure everyone in it is currently active with the company. That takes time. I do weekly video chats on training topics. I send emails distilling information from the company. Sometimes I pay business coaches, social media coaches, etcetera, to put on classes. Usually I'll work with another team leader to do that. And then there's the travel..."

"What do you mean?"

"Glamarosa invites me to speak at events, speak to other teams, do publicity work and be in photo shoots at their offices in New Jersey and on location. It's an honor, really. But it... requires a lot of travel."

"And they don't reimburse you?"

"They do!" Amy looked down. "Or, at least, they're supposed to. But I haven't seen a travel reimbursement for awhile now."

"That's weird."

"It is. I'm sure it's just a mistake, they'll get it fixed. Trust, remember?"

"Right. Trust. What happens when people quit? Could you go down in rose levels?"

"No, it's lifetime sponsored. The only way is up, even if your checks get smaller."

"Huh."

Amy had blended her foundation now and was putting on fake eyelashes. This was a lot of work for a day in workshops.

"I know what you're thinking," Amy said finally. "It's a lot. People outside the business have a hard time understanding it. But it's more than a business. It's a way of life. It's a family. I can't imagine ever not doing Glamarosa. I'm a lifer. I can't think of anything they could do that would make me want to quit."

Sadie was surprised by this monologue. She hadn't been pushing Amy, had she?

"Okay, last question," Sadie said. "What does bringing the husbands home mean?"

Amy laughed. "It means bringing your partner into the business and allowing them to quit their day job."

"What if they like their job? Like Leo? He's a doctor, I can't imagine he's going to leave his job to run a boutique?"

"Maybe not. But it's a goal a lot of women that start doing

well with Glamarosa want to hit, and the Valentines encourage it. And they encourage partners to attend events, get involved in the business."

Sadie opened her mouth to ask another question, but Amy held up her watch. "Breakfast has already started. Let's get dressed, you can ask me more later."

"Fine," Sadie sighed. Her tummy was growling, and she needed coffee. "But first, let's look for those leggings."

Chapter Twelve

Sadie would give it to Glamarosa in one aspect—the clothes were comfortable. She looked like she was going to pose in front of a field of wildflowers with her two-point-five children and bearded husband with two-point-five tattoos for her quarterly lifestyle photo shoot, but she was comfortable as heck.

And apparently that was the look to shoot for, because when she entered the dining room, she was greeted with smiles.

"Looking good, Sadie," Amalia called from the buffet.

Kenna flicked an approving glance. Rosalie nodded encouragingly.

"That Iris skirt is perfect on you!" Lexi chirped from the table. Her eyes were red from crying, and Sadie was glad she could lift her spirits a little.

She glanced down at her chambray ankle length A-line skirt —apparently the style was called Iris—rose-patterned three-quarter length sleeve top, and lightweight cream cardigan. She looked fine. A little fancy for her taste, but fine. And at least she fit in a little now. She needed a pound of silver and gold jewelry, hair that held a curl for longer than ten minutes, hours in a tanning booth, and veneers to really fit in, but at least she wasn't slumping around in her sweatpants while everyone else looked like they'd stepped out of a magazine.

Despite the chipper reactions to her entrance, the mood at the table was solemn, as expected. After Sadie loaded up her plate with fluffy scrambled eggs, sausage, a blueberry muffin she'd baked yesterday and not expected to eat, and fruit, she sat next to Amy, who poured her a cup of coffee.

Amy was tense, pushing her food around on her plate without eating. They hadn't found the leggings in her room. Apparently, she hadn't locked up after herself when she'd delivered everything to her room, so anyone could have snaggged them. She didn't remember if they'd still been there when she'd gone to bed.

Before Sadie could pick up her fork, Glenn asked everyone to bow their heads in honor of Steffy.

"O Lord, we lament the loss of Steffy, our friend and sister. She was a rainbow, a bright sunshine..."

Sadie snuck her eyes open. Everyone's head was bowed, eyes closed. Except for Kenna's, who shrugged and smirked at her.

"...Eternal rest grant unto her, O Lord, and let perpetual light shine upon her. May her soul, through the mercy of God, rest in peace. And O Lord, be with us, as we seek justice for her. Amen."

Everyone ate in silence for a few minutes, forks scraping the plates and coffee being slurped the only sounds.

Finally, Kenna broke the silence.

"I know nobody with Glamarosa would do this," she burst out, dropping her fork dramatically.

"Now Kenna," Glenn started, but she cut him off.

"No! It wasn't any of us, there's no way! We're a family! It had to be someone from outside Glamarosa."

Sadie felt her ears pinking, a sure sign her temper was rising. Rich words from someone who'd skipped the prayer in honor of Steffy moments ago. And, if it wasn't someone from Glamarosa, then Kenna was calling out Sadie, Gavin, Ms. Beatrice, and the documentary crew as the best suspects. How ballsy of her, especially from someone who'd fought with Steffy just last night.

Sadie opened her mouth before she could think better of it.

"Were y'all a family when you were fighting in the hallway outside my room last night?"

Lexi gasped.

Glenn sputtered.

Amy stiffened next to her.

"That's none of your business," Kenna hissed. "That was *family* business."

"You fought with Steffy?" Amalia asked.

"Is that how you got that black eye, Brett? Steffy was a scrappy one." This from Jon Sr, said with a leer at Freddy.

"Be respectful!" Jon Jr chastised his father and uncle.

"Steffy and I had a mild disagreement," Kenna sniffed.

"You accused her of stealing from you and said she punched Brett because he put his hands on her." Amy kicked Sadie under the table and Sadie winced. Maybe she shouldn't be so confrontational. But, then again, Sheriff Wise had asked her to poke around...

"Is this true, Kenna?" Rosalie looked at her with alarm.

Kenna put her napkin on the table, the look she gave Sadie murderous. "I'll discuss this with my *Glamarosa* family, and my Glamarosa family only." She stood and stomped out the door. Brett followed, plate in hand, mouth full of eggs, glaring darkly Sadie.

Glenn cleared his throat, having mopped up the coffee he'd spit on himself. "Sadie, I appreciate you asking questions. It's important that Steffy have justice. I should have told you, dear sisters, about the spat between Steffy and Kenna last night. It was truly a misunderstanding. I showed Steffy to her room afterwards, and she was very remorseful and planning to apologize to Kenna and Brett first thing this morning." His breath hitched. "She never got the opportunity, poor darling."

"Those two have always been touchy with each other," Amalia sniffled into her coffee cup.

"Kenna will regret that the last words she said to her friend were in anger," Rosalie agreed.

If they were the last words she said, Sadie thought. Had Kenna had gone to Steffy's room to continue their argument? To get back what she said Steffy stole? Or even gone back to apologize, to work it out?

Her thoughts were interrupted by the entrance of the film crew, Adam at the back of the pack. Sadie sighed. No one was going to talk with them around.

"Sadie, you're welcome to join us in our general session today," Glenn said.

"Uhhh...I appreciate that, Glenn, really. I think I'll sit it out, though. I have work I brought with me I can get done." *Lie.*

"You can't be alone though, of course," Rosalie insisted.

"Um...I'll hang in the kitchen with Gavin. He was saying he needed help, and I know my way around an industrial kitchen."

Glenn and Rosalie seemed put out, but Sadie shrugged it off. She wanted to do some sleuthing. Maybe she could get Gavin to serve as lookout while she did. Sadie wondered if she should be automatically as trusting as Gavin as she was. Was it that she felt like she knew him from TV? Or the way he'd bravely rushed forward to save the film crew yesterday? Or that she'd seen him at his most vulnerable, during his panic attack? It was probably a combination of all three.

The breakfast broke up after that, but before Sadie could grab a serving dish to take back to the kitchen and beg Gavin to save her from the seminar, Adam sidled up beside her.

"Listen," he said in a low voice. "You need to stay away from Amy Peters."

"What the fuck?" Heads swiveled their direction.

"Jesus, Sadie. Do you know how to whisper?"

"It's not one of my better qualities. What do you mean?" She hissed.

"Just listen to me."

Amy appeared at Sadie's side. "Why are you two talking about me?"

"Adam says I should stay away from you." Too late, she remembered. This wasn't Adam. This was Nick. *Shit.*

"Ugh, Sadie, you're the worst at this." Adam sighed heavily. "Both of you, in the library. We need to talk."

* * *

The library was deserted, again, but it was less welcoming than it'd been last night. Was Mr. Chops above the fireplace grimmer, too?

Adam hustled them in and shut the door behind him, pointedly locking it while looking at Sadie.

Amy had stopped short, turning to peer at Adam warily.

"Wait a second...I recognize you..."

"We met once," Adam admitted.

"Oh yeah!" Sadie clapped, and they both jumped. "My birthday, second year of grad school! You were back in town randomly, Amy, and you would've met there."

"Midnight bowling. Right." Amy laughed, then sobered. "But your name isn't Nick Walker."

"Yeah yeah yeah, we all know that, Amy," Sadie waved that off. "So long story short, Adam, I trust Amy implicitly. Why are you throwing shade at her?"

Adam frowned at Amy. "If Sadie trusts you, Amy, you need to come clean with her."

In front of her eyes, Amy crumpled, going from the confident, bubbly friend she knew to a sobbing mess on the couch.

"It's so bad, Sadie," Amy sobbed.

Sadie sat next to her, heart pounding. What could this be? Amy didn't have it in her to kill Steffy, did she?

"Just tell me, Amy. You can tell me anything." Sadie braced herself.

Amy took a bracing breath and scrubbed her face. "I...I went to Steffy's room last night. I might be the last person that saw her alive!"

"We only have your word for it that she was alive when you left her, though," Adam said, his voice grim.

"How did you know Amy went into her room?"

"I saw her. I was up and I saw her leave the room." Sadie would be asking Adam questions about his nighttime wanderings, but that could wait.

"But you said you found Steffy this morning after you heard a loud noise!"

"Wait, what? I thought Shayna found her!" Amy's jaw had dropped.

"Ah, so you both have secrets to spill. Listen," Sadie snapped her fingers at them. "The three of us are in this together now. Drop the acts, tell me everything, and let's trust each other." *Trust*, like what held together the Glamarosa team.

"Fine," Amy moaned. "I'll go first." She launched into her story.

"Last night, after Steffy stole those leggings from me, I felt bad about the way things went down. When I went up to my room, I moped around about it, tossed and turned in bed. Then I decided I needed to apologize to her. It was around one-thirty. I looked at Facebook and saw she was live, selling stock from her room and about to wrap it up, so I asked her if I could come by, and she said yes."

"She was selling out of her room in the middle of the night?" *What commitment*, Sadie thought.

"She was famously a night owl. A lot of her customers were shift workers, nurses, people like that. She would go live at midnight and sell more than I could in prime time."

"Okay...but why not wait until the morning to talk to her?" Sadie wouldn't have wanted a text that late, no matter how silly the fight had been.

"I felt like I needed to apologize before the seminar started in the morning. She and I were supposed to be presenting ideas to streamline team management together, and I didn't want to go into that without clearing the air between us."

"But why even apologize? What did you really do? You had your hand on the leggings first."

"Sadie, let her tell her story," Adam groused.

"Fine. Continue."

Amy sat up straighter. "I did have my hand on the leggings first. They were mine. I wasn't going to give them back, and I didn't." She made big eyes at Sadie. The leggings weren't missing in her room because she'd given them to Steffy. "But I shouldn't have disrespected her that way, not in front of the Valentines. She's a big seller, and I need to be respectful."

"So you went to her room..."

"Yeah. I went to her room. She was still dressed, and agitated, had just wrapped up her live sale. She didn't say anything about the conflict with Kenna and Brett. I didn't know about that until this morning. I told her I was sorry that I'd been disrespectful, and she accepted my apology. We chatted for a bit, just girl talk, and talked about our presentation we had planned, and then I left her. It was about two-fifteen when I left."

"Did you see anyone on your way back to your room?"

Amy looked at Adam pointedly. "I did not. But apparently I was seen."

"Alright Adam. Now you need to spill."

"I was up scouting filming locations for the next morning," he said.

Sadie interrupted him. "Nope. Start at the beginning. Why are you here filming a documentary when the last I knew you were launching a startup? Why the false name? Is your crew in on this too?"

A muscle ticked in Adam's jaw and he frowned off into the distance, as if calculating what he could share.

"You said trust, Adam. I need to understand what's going on to be able to do that."

"Fine." He sighed heavily. "I had a friend get involved with Glamarosa. She lost everything. I told her it was a bad idea, that the customer of a multi-level marketing company is the consultant, so they don't care about their sales to customers–" Amy made a disgruntled noise, but didn't interrupt. "And that not controlling her products, being tied to only one retailer, was a hard place to be in business. But she didn't listen, and in the end, she lost everything to it. Her home, her relationships, her–" he broke off, swallowed hard. "I did some research into the company, and realized there are inconsistencies in their business plans, in the few financials they've released. As a family-owned company, they don't have to provide much. I was talking it over with my buddy Alex, who really is a documentarian, and he had this idea to approach them to film a documentary, that we'd be able to get behind the scenes and maybe get enough information on them we could expose what scammers they are."

"Oh, give me a break!" Amy burst out then. "All businesses have people that fail. A lot of businesses have one wholesaler they're beholden too—have you ever been in an Apple store? A Nike store? I'm sorry for your friend, but the Valentines aren't scammers. It's a legitimate business model, and the sellers here are proof of that."

"Y'all can argue about the ins and outs of this later," Sadie said. "So Alex is in on this with you, and Sam? But why the false name?"

"If you google Adam Stroop, there's lots of info about my startup. Nick Walker is general enough it wouldn't be surprising to not find anything about me. Alex and Sam gave me a crash course in filming and set me up as the producer. It was honestly...incredibly easy to get Glamarosa to agree to this. A minimum of paperwork, and they gave us full access, and agreed they didn't have final approval of whatever we show in the film. Or series. It might be a series. I have one streaming network interested already."

"I should tell them what you're up to." Amy stood up and started to pace. "This is what they mean when they talk about trust. If I don't tell them, I'm breaking their confidence in me."

"You can't, Amy," Sadie frowned at Adam. "Maybe yesterday, I would've told you to expose them. It's not ethical, what you're doing," she directed at Adam. "And you're not a journalist. I don't know if you're covered by journalistic ethics, but I can guarantee even my ethically wishy-washy journalist friend Penny would have a problem with this. But you can't tell on them now, Amy. Not when there's been a murder, and having the crew here might help expose the killer. This is serious business."

"And so is Glamarosa." Amy stopped pacing and turned to

them, her face set. "I won't tell on you, and I won't interfere, but I don't want any part of this. Consider my film release rescinded. Now, I have to go to my seminar. I have to give a presentation without Steffy." She sniffled. "But I'll let you know if I hear anything." And with that, she turned and walked out the door, her neon pink lace duster cardigan swinging behind her.

Chapter Thirteen

Sadie found Chef Gavin in the kitchen, muttering darkly as he shoved dishes into the commercial dishwasher basket.

"Please tell me you hate doing dishes and you need an assistant, and I can help you instead of attending the Glamarosa seminar today?"

He dropped a pot into the basket and turned a mega-watt grin on her. "You're a saint, Sadie Moose. I'm supposed to be serving sushi for lunch today, and I'll never get it done if I don't start now."

She glanced down at her fancy clothes and grimaced. "Okay, I'm going to run upstairs and change, and then I'll be down to be your kitchen bitch. Sushi sounds great."

She turned to leave, but he stopped her. "Wait, you're not supposed to be alone!"

"Neither are you, my dude," she sighed. "Get to work. I'll be fine."

The seminar was set up in a meeting room off the stairs, and Sadie peeked in as she walked by. For reasons she couldn't fathom, they were...dancing. Upbeat music pumped, and everyone in the room, even Paul the lawyer, was dancing. But though the music was upbeat, and the dancing was enthusiastic, Sadie saw tears in Amalia's eyes as she twirled. Amy's face was blank. Jon Jr's eyes were red. It was a disturbing tableau, but even as she watched for another full minute, they continued to dance.

Sadie shuddered, then tore her eyes away and slipped past the door, wondering what, exactly, was up with Glamarosa.

* * *

Back in her room, Sadie changed into a pair of leggings and a Moose's Bakery t-shirt, as well as her sensible walking shoes. Just the thought of open-toed sandals in the kitchen made her shudder. Glancing at her watch, she decided Gavin could struggle for a few more minutes, and she unzipped her suitcase pocket and pulled out Steffy's planner.

Sadie sat in the chair Adam had collapsed into earlier, tucked her feet underneath her, and opened the planner. The first section was a calendar, with monthly two-page spreads, and then weekly two-page spreads following each month. The pages were decorated with Glamarosa flowers and pithy boss babe sayings like, "work hard, play hard" and "bloom where you are planted" and "wake up and hustle". Steffy's schedule was packed. Glancing through the last four months, Sadie saw she'd traveled across the country many times for Glamarosa events. Philadelphia. Miami. Boise. Fargo. Vegas. Anchorage. Houston. When she wasn't traveling for an event, her in-home boutique was booked with parties and private shopping appointments. And, every day, usually in the late evenings, but sometimes during the day on the weekends, she'd written GO LIVE on her schedule. It looked exhausting. Sadie couldn't see a single day where she hadn't had something work-related planned. She tried to see if there was anything suspicious about the meetings and conference calls and zooms peppered throughout the schedule, but nothing stood out.

The second half of the book was a notebook and sales planner. Sadie's eyes popped wide when she saw where Steffy had charted her monthly sales numbers. She was doing big business. And, though it was a smaller number, her bonus checks were high, too. There was a list of names she'd titled "Follow Ups", but nothing jumped out at Sadie. She flipped through a few more pages, conscious of time passing. She didn't want to bear the brunt of Chef Gavin's famous temper.

Bingo.

Steffy had, in rainbow-colored inks, headed a list "ENEMIES OF GLAMAROSA".

On it were a few names Sadie didn't recognize, and a few she did. Kenna and Brett Ward. Shayna and Julie McCoy. And, shockingly: Rosalie Valentine.

* * *

Half an hour later, aproned and elbow deep in the sink as she washed a pot that wouldn't fit in the industrial dishwasher, Sadie's mind whirled with the information she'd learned from Steffy's planner.

Was the list a joke? How could something written in rainbows and embellished with stars be serious? But if Rosalie, the McCoy sisters, or Kenna found the list...Sadie was sure they would take it seriously. What would it take for Steffy to put them on that list? The conversation Sadie had overheard last night with Adam seemed so far away now, though it had only been about twelve hours. What had been said? The man had called the situation bullshit. The woman had called it bad luck.

There'd been kissy noises. Then the man said, "without the Joneses here, I don't think we can make our move."

The Joneses. Also on that list had been Sarajane and Matt Jones. The couple that hadn't made it up the mountain. Sadie was staying in their suite.

And then the woman had replied, "We don't need them. We have the McCoy sisters."

Who were on the list.

So who had been in that room last night? Rosalie and her husband Freddy? Sadie had barely seen them look at each other. She didn't think they'd be making kissy noises by the fireplace. And at the end of the encounter, the woman had said she needed to get back so she wouldn't be missed, which had made Sadie think the liaison was illicit.

The only man on the list was Brett Ward. If he hadn't been with a McCoy sister, that left either Rosalie or his wife. Unless Steffy hadn't identified another enemy? And what would that mean, anyway? And what move were they talking about? Some sort of hostile takeover of the business? Rosalie was already at the head of the company, why would they need to do a hostile takeover?

It was all so confusing.

Sadie pulled the drains on the sinks and stripped off her rubber gloves, blowing hair off her sweaty brow.

Gavin was, as usual, grumbling behind her.

She turned and leaned up against a dry part of the counter. "Aren't you used to working under a time limit, Mr. Top Chef?"

Gavin flashed her a grin, then went back to concentrating on cutting vegetables in precise strips. "Are you going to yell, 'utensils down, hands up!' at me before lunchtime?"

"Maybe," Sadie laughed. "You know that van I drove up here? I won it in a reality show this winter."

"Really?" Gavin looked at her, surprised. "It's already aired?"

"Well, no," Sadie said. "They delivered the vans same day I found out I'd been on the show."

Gavin put his knife down and dried his hands on a towel, pondering her. "That's strange. I've been on a few other reality cooking competitions, and I've never received my prize before my episode aired. I have a buddy who was on a show that got pulled before it aired because one of the judges was exposed for being a serial sexual harasser, and even though he won, he never got his prize."

Ugh. Sadie had known something about that reality show wasn't quite right. But what was the scam? How was she being played? "Weird," Sadie agreed. She tried to shake it off. There was enough weirdness happening in this chalet, she didn't need to think about it now. "What else can I do to help you?"

Gavin picked his knife back up and pushed a pile of cucumber strips to the side of his cutting board, then set in to dissect a carrot. "I'm on track for lunch service. You tackling the dishes was very helpful. If we don't get out of here tonight, I might need you to bake more muffins or something for tomorrow's breakfast."

"I'll check the pantry and see what I can come up with," Sadie said. She looked out the window over Gavin's shoulder. The snow was still coming down. "This is all pretty wild, huh? How did you get wrapped up in it?"

"I'm not. And neither are you, right?" He cocked an eyebrow at her.

Sadie grimaced. "I'm always in the middle, it feels like. My nosy nature."

Gavin harrumphed. He pushed the precisely cut carrot sticks to the side and started on an apple. "Glenn's a fan of the show. I'm between restaurants, trying to figure out my next venture, and I couldn't pass up the money he offered to come cook this week. Travel paid, too."

"This whole experience must be costing them a fortune."

"I'm pretty expensive."

"So am I," Sadie winked. "I guess business really is going well?"

Gavin put down his knife again and leaned on the counter behind him, evidently resolved that he wasn't going to get more work done until he'd blabbed with her. "It's either going really well, or really bad."

"You mean they might be paying all this money to make people believe things are going well, when they aren't?"

"Bingo. I used to work as a private chef before I was at Radis," he name-dropped the James-Beard-award-winning French restaurant in LA like it was nothing, "and you could always tell the difference between customers that were really doing well, and customers that were trying to show how well they were doing in order to get more financing for their ventures."

"Do you have an indicator of how Glamarosa is doing?"

"Well, according to the news, they're not doing too well. Sales are down. They laid off some employees last winter, right before Christmas, which didn't go over well in the press. They're involved in a big lawsuit with their overseas manufacturer. Glenn continues to insist that these are all misunderstandings, but they didn't put out a first quarter report this year."

"You've done your homework." Sadie narrowed her eyes at him.

He shrugged. "I just won a major cooking competition. I'm under scrutiny right now. I didn't want to take a job that might cast a stain on my reputation."

"And yet you decided to come work here, knowing there was a film crew, and weird things afoot with their business?"

Gavin sighed. "Well...an all-expense paid trip to Jackson Hole was hard to pass up. I'd love to open something up here, you know."

Sadie's interest was piqued. "Like at the resort?"

"I think in town. I found out there's a restaurant the owners are looking to sell."

Sadie thought about it. "Oh, the Carloni's! Maybe? They're my neighbors. I know the business hasn't been doing that well, and they were considering selling their home to float the restaurant costs until things improved. Last time I was there the place was empty, though the food was good."

"Sometimes restaurants just fall out of favor. It's not necessarily because of bad food or service, they just haven't innovated to meet the current interests."

"And old school Italian food..."

"Well, the Valentine's would love it," Gavin laughed. "But I'm not surprised they're looking to get out."

"Are you really thinking about buying Carloni's?"

He sobered. "I'm considering it. I need to go check out the location, check out the town."

"So you might be a new neighbor of mine, then."

"Wouldn't be bad to start out with a friend in the business."

Sadie's chest filled with warmth. She liked Gavin Vincent. She hoped he would move to Jackson and help enliven the restaurant scene. Maybe she could work out a deal to provide his pastries or desserts in exchange for something on her menu, or just to build clout. Plus she had contacts with the best coffee roaster, the best brewery, the best farmers...And perhaps more of his Chef Off friends would visit, too. Sadie could picture the TikToks now.

"Well, if I'm a friend," Sadie said, "it's probably time for me to come clean with you."

"You killed Steffy Austin?" He joked.

"Nope. Did you?"

"Nope."

"Well, want to help me find out who did?"

Chapter Fourteen

It took a little explaining, and Gavin took a large step back from her when Sadie explained this wasn't her first time encountering a dead body, but eventually, he came around to helping her investigate. As she helped him roll fresh spring rolls, she explained what she knew so far, leaving out the tidbits about Adam and Amy for now, but explaining that Sheriff Wise had asked her to sleuth.

"That's the most small town thing I've ever heard," Gavin snorted.

"When you live in a valley that frequently gets cut off from the outside world in the winter due to avalanches, you learn to use the resources you have at your fingertips," Sadie explained. It *was* strange. But these were strange times.

They finished the spring rolls and Gavin got her the ingredients to make a peanut sauce, then told her how to make it while he started crafting the sushi rolls.

"So what I need is a buddy that can watch out for me while I sneak around," Sadie explained while using a small spatula to scoop out a spoon full of honey.

Gavin considered that while he assembled a spicy tuna roll. "So you need a lookout."

"Sure, a lookout."

"And where are we going to snoop?"

"Investigate. Snooping has such a negative connotation. Remember, we're the good guys. I'd like to look around in rooms, if I can."

"They're probably all locked. Don't tell me you brought a lock-picking kit, Nancy Drew."

"I don't usually pack it when I'm headed to Mexico on vacation," Sadie quipped, dunking a tasting spoon in the sauce and holding it out for Gavin to try.

"More hoisin," he instructed after he tasted.

"They might not be locked. Won't know if we don't try. Everyone's supposed to be in this seminar until one, so say I helped you wrap this up and put it in the fridge by eleven-thirty, that would give us an hour to go snoop."

"Only if you promise to make breakfast treats for tomorrow."

"Done."

"And introduce me to your best suppliers."

"Done."

"And let me take you out to dinner when you get back."

Sadie glanced up at him, and he winked at her. "I bat for the other team, but I like taking friends out to dinner. Plus I need to scope out the competition."

Perfect. Meet an amazing man, find out he's gay. Just my kind of luck.

"Those were all things I'd planned, anyway. Sounds like you just signed up to be my sidekick."

"Lookout, Sadie. A lookout. It's an important distinction."

They rushed through their prep then, Sadie putting together more sauces and helping Gavin arrange the rolls on platters. She piped wasabi with a flourish to Gavin's approval. After sliding everything in the fridge to wait until lunch and a quick cleanup, they were ready to go.

But as they started to sneak upstairs, a cold voice stopped them.

* * *

"Just where do you think you two are going?"

Sadie stopped short and whirled around to see Ms. Beatrice standing at the bottom of the stairs, frowning.

"There you are," Gavin improvised. "We were worried about you. You don't have a buddy."

She softened slightly. "I know this chalet like the house I grew up in. I don't need a buddy. I'd hear anyone coming."

"That's reassuring," Sadie said. "I was just going to go change for lunch, and Gavin said he'd come wait outside my door since my buddy is in the seminar."

Ms. Beatrice climbed one step, so she was even with Sadie, then leaned in closer. "You're terrible at snooping, Ms. Moose."

Drat. Caught.

"But I promised Sheriff Wise I would help you. I suppose you've roped in Gavin?"

Sadie blinked at her. Of course Sheriff Wise would inform Ms. Beatrice she was going to be snooping around. She was kind of the boss? Or Glenn was? As her ex, wildland firefighter Jake, would have said, the chain of command was murky.

"She sure has," Gavin said conspiratorially. "So I guess our crime fighting duo just became a trio. Hmm. I can't think of any detectives with two sidekicks."

"Lookouts," Sadie corrected. "Phriney Fischer? She has her lady's maid, her two chauffeurs, her butler...well, I guess her whole household staff are kind of her sidekicks."

"Either way, if you please," Ms. Beatrice said, obviously over the conversation, "let's go upstairs. I have the keys. You'll have to be quick."

Sadie sped up the stairs, not quite believing her ears. Was she really going to be let into everyone's rooms? What was she actually looking for? This was a huge opportunity. She couldn't mess this up.

On the second floor, the three of them hustled past the first door in the hallway, which was Sadie's suite. "I left something in there for you," Ms. Beatrice said cryptically as they passed it.

"The planner?"

Ms. Beatrice frowned. "What planner? No. The witness statements. They're under your mattress. You should make your bed. Sloppy."

Sadie rolled her eyes behind the stern woman's back. She'd need to retreat into her room to read those as soon as she could.

"This is Jon Jr's room," Ms. Beatrice said, stopping in front of the next door. "Gavin, you go watch the stairs, I'll watch the hallway in case someone is in their rooms. If someone's coming, hoot."

"Like...an owl?" Gavin looked perplexed.

"That's not a natural sound you'd hear inside, is it?" Sadie agreed. "Can you chime instead? Make grandfather clock sounds? There's a grandfather clock in the sitting room."

"Perhaps make an iPhone alarm sound?"

"Cough twice?"

"This is all a game to you two," Ms. Beatrice sniffed. "A guest has been *murdered* and for whatever reason, you're supposed to figure out who it was. We're hooting. End of story." She unlocked the door and pushed Sadie through it. "You have five minutes," she hissed.

* * *

Five minutes to look for evidence that Jon Jr was a murderer. That hardly seemed like enough time. But she'd have to make it work.

Taking a deep breath, then coughing when she inhaled the cologne Jon Jr must douse on himself, she walked straight to the bed. Nothing in the bedside table. Nothing shoved under the mattress. A suitcase was open on the bench at the end of the bed and clothes spilled out of it messily. Careful not to make a noticeable difference in the disarray, Sadie rummaged through it, finding nothing of use. She checked the desk, then the closet. Jon Jr must have been planning to ski later this week because his boots and ski clothes were piled in one corner of it. Spying the suit jacket Jon Jr had worn the night before, she reached into the pockets, then gasped when she felt the distinctive cold steel of a small pistol.

She pulled her hand out of the pocket and backed up. *Woah.* Now, this was Wyoming. Chances were someone would be concealed carrying here. But Jon Jr? She hadn't pegged him for a CCW type. Why would he need a gun, here, surrounded by family and retailers for the corporation he worked for, most of which he knew well? Her phone buzzed. Her four minute and thirty second timer was up, meaning she had time for one last look around. Frowning, she stepped back to the closet and turned on her phone flashlight, taking a photo of the gun in the pocket, just in case it was important later. She patted the other pockets, then checked the shoes lined up on the floor, and then her time was up.

So, Jon Jr had a gun, but nothing else that pointed to him having a grudge against Steffy. Also, nothing that showed he was having an affair with Steffy, like Amy had insinuated. Nothing of hers was in the room, no pictures of them together... of course, those would probably be on his phone or his laptop, which he must have with him, because they weren't in his room.

She stepped outside and shut the door behind her, using her shirt to grab the door. If the cops fingerprinted this place eventually, hers would be everywhere. Another reason to find the real killer.

Ms. Beatrice locked the door, and they moved on to the next.

"The lawyer Paul," she intoned, swinging the door open.

Sadie set her phone timer, then swept into the room.

* * *

Half an hour later, exhausted and mind whirling, Sadie, Ms. Beatrice and Gavin crowded into Sadie's room to go over what she'd found.

"You are kind of messy," Gavin said, nose scrunched as he sat in a chair by the window. He gestured at the bed. "Cute pillow though. Why didn't I get one of those?"

Sadie picked up Flower and snuggled it against her chest.

"You're in Chef's quarters," Ms. Beatrice explained succinctly.

"So get him a stuffed carrot or a pig or something," Sadie suggested. Ms. Beatrice huffed.

Sadie had found a whole lot of nothing.

On the second floor, The McCoy sisters had left their planners in their room, and Sadie had thought she'd found a jackpot, but aside from a bunch of canceled parties and a long list of retailers with their names methodically crossed out, she didn't find anything suspicious in them. Nothing as glaring as a list of enemies, at least. She wondered again what incident the sisters had been involved in. She wished her phone would work so she could Google it.

The lawyer Paul had left his room neat as a pin, his suitcase zipped up in the closet, his clothes neatly put away in drawers and the closet. Sadie hadn't found anything out of the ordinary in his room.

The Wards had more luggage than Sadie could sift through in five minutes and a taste for expensive skin products.

The film crew's rooms were sparse, with equipment spread throughout them.

They'd obviously skipped Steffy's suite, which was, in fact, across from Adam's.

On the third floor, Amalia and Rosalie and their husbands had the two largest suites. Glenn took up the next largest, then the Bautistas, McCoys, and Titus each had a suite, each more spacious than the second floor, where they'd crowded in eight total rooms instead of six.

Titus had boxes of Glamarosa product piled in his room, along with painstakingly accessorized outfits arranged in the closet. His ironing board, iron, and steamer had all recently been used. His wallet had been left in the pocket of his jacket, and the license inside stated his real name was Derrick Ross and he was from Kansas. Titus was definitely a cooler name.

The Bautista's room was a mess, with clothes on the floor and the bed ripped apart. A bottle of melatonin gummies for sleeping were on the bedside table, but again, Sadie found nothing out of the normal. They seemed like a couple that didn't get away from their kids often and were enjoying their adult-only giveaway.

Sadie had found nothing out of the obvious in any of the Valentines, rooms, either. Though she had found it interesting there were two beds in Rosalie and Freddy's suite, both of them having been slept in. Maybe one of them was just a restless sleeper, though. A C-PAP machine had been on one bedside table in Amalia and Jonathan's suite, and Sadie wondered which one used it. Would their partner notice if someone snuck out in the night while they were wearing one? Sadie wondered about Glenn. Why was he alone? Did he have a partner? He was a handsome man, charming. Sadie needed to ask Amy, though it seemed more curiosity than being a part of the murder investigation.

It was frustrating, though she wasn't sure what she had expected to find. A diary with a description of the crime in it? But surely there was *something* that could lead her to the killer.

She hadn't investigated Amy's suite, since she'd already been in it and would be in it again. She wondered about Gavin's stuffed-animal-free chef's quarters, and about the apartment Ms. Beatrice lived in. She supposed she'd have to investigate them next, but it made her depressed to think about it.

Ms. Beatrice pulled the brick-like satellite phone from her fanny pack and dialed Sheriff Wise.

They didn't have much to report and hung up quickly. Sadie wondered if she should've told him about the gun, about the list of enemies, about Kenna's smirk during the prayer for Steffy, but really what did any of those things add up to? A whole lot of nothing, at least so far.

Dejected, Gavin and Sadie headed down the stairs to get lunch set up in the dining room, but Ms. Beatrice pulled her aside, pressing a key in her hand.

"Don't touch anything in there," she said. "Use a lookout."

Sadie stared down at the key. It was for the Prospector's Suite. Steffy's room.

Chapter Fifteen

Sadie's heart was still beating fast when she joined everyone for lunch. The key to Steffy's room was heavy in her pocket. Belatedly, when she saw Amy's crestfallen look, she realized she was still in her kitchen clothes. This dress code was a pain.

Shrugging it off, she piled a plate with the lunch she'd helped Gavin with, then sat next to Amy, who was frowning at a spring roll.

"How was your morning?" Sadie asked brightly.

Amy dropped the spring roll. "It was fine. Just fine."

"Doesn't sound like it was fine," Sadie popped a California roll in her mouth.

Amy glanced around the room. They were sitting a few chairs away from anyone else, and the hum of conversation flowed around them. She leaned her head into Sadie so their conversation wouldn't be overheard. "It was so weird, Sadie. They just...pretended nothing had happened to Steffy."

Sadie pulled a face.

"It's just like everything else in this company," Amy grumbled, on a roll now. "They just smooth any problems over with platitudes, with pithy sayings, with *trust*, by pivoting it around to somehow be *your fault*." She picked the spring roll back up and took a big bite, like she was trying to staunch the flow of words. Sadie had never heard Amy be so candid about Glamarosa. It was usually that everything was fantastic, no matter what Sadie saw in the news about the company.

"That's awkward, and weird, Amy. I'm sorry. Is there anything I can do to make this better for you?"

Amy swallowed her bite and took a drink of her seltzer. "Find out who did this. And...if there's something going on with Glamarosa, I want to know about that, too. I've given enough of my time and money to a company that's this...fishy." She poked at the salmon nigiri on her plate as she said it, and Sadie's stomach turned.

Right. She needed to focus. She needed to talk to some more people. Maybe she could solve this thing without having to go into Steffy's room. Ugh. She pushed her plate away, appetite gone. She glanced around the room. Titus was walking towards the table, his plate piled with food. Sadie gestured to the open chair next to her, smiling. His brow furrowed, but he came towards them, sinking into the chair.

"How are you, Titus?" *Derrick Ross from Kansas*, Sadie said silently in her head.

"Pretty messed up, actually," he said, frowning down at his plate. "Steffy was...she was special. We'd been working on a project together, and now I'm worried what will happen to it." *Pretty self-involved of him*, Sadie thought, *to be worried about the project when Steffy was dead.*

Amy perked up at that. "What was it, Titus?"

Titus looked around the room, then leaned in closer to the two of them. Apparently it was a *secret* project. "A higher end line. Higher price points, more luxury, more style. We were going to launch it as a holiday line, with the hope of moving it into mainline based on its success."

"Huh. Higher price points? My ladies already don't like spending forty dollars for tops. Some women tell me their Glamarosa dresses are the most expensive they've bought since their wedding dress."

Titus shrugged. "It'll be so fantastic, they won't care how much it is. They'll buy it."

"Who will?" Sadie asked. "Your customers, or Amy's?"

Titus's gaze sharpened on Sadie. "They're the same."

"Are they? Aren't your customers actually the retailers? I'm sure they'll buy it if that's what's available, but what if they can't sell it to their customers?" Amy kicked Sadie under the table, but she didn't let up. "Glamarosa probably wouldn't care, I guess?"

"The success of our retailers is the most important thing to us. We're changing families, bettering home lives," Titus said, parroting the company line.

"Why did Steffy get to work on that with you?"

Titus shoved a spicy salmon roll in his mouth and chewed, buying himself time.

"Was it because she used to be a designer herself? I heard she was on Next Fashion Star," Sadie pushed.

"She was?" Amy said, shocked. "I never knew that! When?"

"I'm not sure," Sadie said. "She mentioned it yesterday in front of Glenn when I was talking to him about the reality TV show I was on."

"Huh," Amy said, pondering her plate, lost in thought.

Titus cleared his throat. "I don't know about her being on that show, but she was the number six retailer in the company," he said, like that should mean something to Sadie.

"Like sixth most profitable?"

"No, like her consultant number was literally six. She didn't have an upline, she was at the very top of her team. And aside from her seniority, she had a great eye. Amalia suggested she work with me to develop the line after I pitched it since she had so many customers and knew what they were looking for."

Something about what Titus said about Steffy's seniority was blaring in her brain, but she couldn't pinpoint what her question was. Before she could untangle it, Amalia came rushing into the room, Rosalie hot on her heels.

"Is Jon Jr in here?" Amalia asked, her voice shrill. Her normally perfect hair had been swept haphazardly into a bun and sweat was beading on her brow.

Everyone looked around. Jon Jr was, obviously, not there.

"What's wrong?" Glenn asked with concern.

"He's not anywhere! Who was his buddy?"

"Uh, me," Paul said nervously. He had soy sauce splattered on his tie. "After the seminar, he said he needed to go up to his room, but I should come get food. Freddy was headed upstairs at the same time, so he said he didn't need a buddy."

Freddy pinkened from where he sat next to Kenna, where they'd been chatting animatedly. "I...I forgot I was supposed to wait for him, I guess. I grabbed what I needed from my room and came right back down."

"Oh no!" Amalia cried, and Rosalie caught her in her arms before she could slump to the floor.

So many people fainting this weekend, Sadie thought. "So he's missing?" she asked. "Where have you looked? Could he just be in the bathroom?"

"We've looked everywhere," Rosalie said, handing Amalia over to her husband, who looked panicked.

"Did he seem okay during your meeting?" Sadie asked.

Everyone looked around at each other. "I...guess?" Kenna said. "None of us are really okay, you know. This is such a tragedy."

Sadie barely kept from rolling her eyes. Glamarosa wasn't treating it like much of a tragedy, what with the dancing and the continued business talk.

"Film dudes, did you see him at any point?" Sadie asked, addressing the now-almost-background camera crew in the room. Adam met her eyes, frowning.

"We haven't seen him since he went upstairs," he said, and Alex and Sam nodded along with him.

"Well, we need to split up and see if we can find him," Sadie declared, standing.

"Yes!" Jonathan said, Amalia safely deposited in a chair, tears leaving trails through her caked-on powder on her cheeks.

"He'll probably come sauntering in here any moment," Freddy protested, gesturing at the platters full of ever-warming sushi.

"If it was your son, you'd be screaming for us to help," Jonathan shouted. Freddy swallowed hard, but nodded.

"You're right, brother. And you're right, Ms. Moose. Let's go find him."

They broke off into pairs. Rosalie was going to stay in the dining room with Amalia, who wasn't up for a search. Gavin and Ms. Beatrice were in the kitchen already, and would be asked to help while Freddy and Jonathan headed outside to look around. Sadie, Amy, and Adam would search the first floor. Titus, Paul, Shayna, and Julie would search the second floor. The Bautistas and Brett and Kenna would search the third floor. Alex and Sam would be filming throughout the house.

Grimly, they broke off to search. As they crept down the hall towards the library, calls of "Jon Jr?" echoing around them, Sadie braced herself for the worst.

* * *

When they entered the library, Adam locked the door behind them.

"Déjà vu," Sadie sighed, looking around. If possible, the library was even grimmer than it had been that morning. It was cold, the fire long dead, the curtains drawn against the depressing continued onslaught of snow outside. Mr. Chops glowered at them.

"What'd you find out this morning?" Adam asked.

"Zip."

"Seriously?"

"Seriously."

Amy frowned. "Speak for yourself. I found something out."

Sadie whirled around at her. "What? And you're just now saying something? Spill it!"

"I didn't think about it until we were talking to Titus. That new line they're talking about...it's total bullshit. Glamarosa has always been about affordability. What do my clients need with luxurious items? Ball gowns? You know who will buy it? Retailers. For themselves. Because I bet Glamarosa makes their dress codes even more intense."

"Wait, there's a formal dress code? I thought you were just picky."

"Oh, no, it's at least three pieces of Glamarosa for all events, leggings are looked down upon for anything formal."

"No wonder you've been on me about my outfits," Sadie mused, glancing down at her non-Glamarosa leggings and t-shirt.

"Can you get to the point, Amy?" Adam sounded exasperated.

"Right. Steffy was number six in the company. The sixth consultant. She didn't have an upline. So what's going to happen to Team Rainbow Shimmer?"

"What...?"

Amy waved a hand. "That's just the name of her team. Get over it. There's over 10,000 consultants on it. That's a *hefty* leadership paycheck every month. Normally, if a consultant leaves the business, her downline rolls up. But Steffy's won't roll up, because Amalia, Rosalie, and Glenn aren't retailers."

Sadie snapped her fingers. "Yes! I was trying to figure something like this out in my head earlier when we were talking to Titus. Will it roll down?"

Amy shook her head. "There's over thirty girls in Steffy's immediate downline. I suppose they could go to the most senior, but I know two or three of those signed on the same day. The competition...would be fierce."

"Is anyone here on her team?"

"Team Rainbow Shimmer?"

Adam grumbled again, and the two women ignored him.

"Actually...the Bautistas are. They're new to the company, they've only been active a year, but they had a big following before from a blog or something, so they grew fast. But they're far, far down in her team. Lots of layers."

A movement out of the corner of Sadie's eye made her jump, and that made Adam and Amy jump.

"Did that curtain just move?" Adam asked in a low voice.

"Shit. Yes." *You, especially, should've thought to look there before talking.* Sadie cursed inwardly.

Together, they advanced on the curtain. Sadie took a deep breath before gripping the edge. She looked at Amy and Adam, who nodded at her.

She ripped the curtain open, expecting someone to spring out at them any moment.

Instead, an icy blast of snowy air swept into the room, taking her breath away.

"What the hell?" Adam said.

Sadie climbed onto the window seat to look out the window.

Snow swirled against a gray sky. In the accumulated snow beneath the window were ski tracks headed away from the lodge and down the hill.

"I think we found Jon Jr," Sadie sighed. "Or, we found how he got out of here, at least."

* * *

The group assembled in the library, alternately looking out the window at the ski tracks and exclaiming about what a stupid thing Jon Jr had done. Ms. Beatrice had gone into his room, confirming his ski boots and clothes Sadie had secretly seen earlier were gone. He'd stored his skis downstairs in the back entry, where there were racks for skis and boots to dry after a long day on the slopes, and they were gone too.

Somehow, without being seen, he'd changed and gathered his things, snuck down the stairs, grabbed his skis, and slipped out the window, skiing down into...what?

"Was he an experienced backcountry skier?" Sadie asked no one in particular.

"He liked to ski at Aspen," Amalia said, white-faced. "We took the kids every year growing up." Sadie guessed that was a no, then.

What would cause him to ski off like that, into a complete unknown? While there was lots of snow at this elevation, it was possible it was raining lower in the valley, and he could run out of snow. Plus, the conditions were ripe for an avalanche with the late season snowpack first being rained on, then covered in heavy, wet, spring snow. What was he running from? Running to?

"Well, I guess that solves our murder then," Kenna mused. She sat in one of the chairs near the still-dark fireplace.

"Kenna!" Brett's eyes were wide, flickering at Amalia, as he protested.

"My nephew is no killer," Glenn said sternly.

"Why else would he run?" Kenna studied her fingernails.

"He must have known something we didn't," Jonathan said, staring out the window forlornly. "I wish he would've told me what he was thinking. I could have gone with him."

"Didn't you say it was a death wish to go out skiing yesterday?" Kenna pointed at Sadie, one long, fuchsia fingernail straight to her chest.

Sadie shrugged. "I'm not an expert, but yeah, it's a bad idea to ski out of here without being familiar with the local terrain, with the avalanche conditions, without backcountry experience...there's no snow in the bottom of the valley, or at least there wasn't yesterday. He'll have a hike ahead of him if he makes it to the bottom."

Amalia sobbed and Sadie wished she'd chosen her words more carefully.

Had he taken his gun with him?

Sadie needed to get back in his room. Maybe he'd left his laptop behind, too. Had Jon Jr killed Steffy in a lover's spat, then used the leggings to make it look like someone else, probably Amy, had done it? Had he then panicked and decided risking the unknown was better than waiting to be questioned by the sheriff when they were eventually rescued?

Or maybe he knew who had killed Steffy, and he knew he was next.

Sadie surveyed the faces in the library. If Jon Jr wasn't the killer, and was instead the next victim...with him gone, who would be next?

Chapter Sixteen

After much discussion, and Amalia and Jonathan retiring to their room as they were beside themselves, Glenn declared that everyone from Glamarosa would go back to their meeting room until dinner.

"We're safer together," he declared.

Ms. Beatrice said she'd alert the sheriff.

Sadie looked around at Ms. Beatrice and Gavin. They were not with Glamarosa, and it felt like Glenn had just made them sitting ducks. But oh well...they could use that time to sleuth, anyway.

Despite Glenn's declaration, the library didn't clear out quickly. Sadie saw the Bautistas huddled together in the corner and decided now was as good a time as any to go ask them some questions.

"This is all just terrible, isn't it?" Sadie asked as she drifted up to them.

"It really is," Lexi sniffled. "This is our first Glamarosa retreat...we never expected anything like this."

"If I could get us out of here, I would," Leo grumbled. "I had my doubts about this operation, Lexi–"

"Please don't start," she hissed. She looked pointedly at Sadie.

Leo shrugged. "She's not with these fanatics. She probably sees the same thing I see. Incompetence."

Sadie gulped. Apparently Leo wasn't a Glamarosa fan. "I have my concerns about the business model," she admitted. "What drew you to join, Lexi?"

Lexi sighed and leaned into her husband, who wrapped an arm around her tenderly. At least they had each other here. The other couples all seemed to be, if not at odds, at least not very affectionate. Kenna seemed to despise Brett. Jonathan ignored Amalia unless she was fainting. She hadn't seen Freddy and Rosalie so much as glance at each other since this morning when he'd comforted her in the great room.

"I had a successful mom blog," Lexi confessed. "I'm kind of...an influencer, I guess? I wanted to branch out into my own clothing line, but it was a lot of work with designers and manufacturers and prototypes and on and on and on. I decided to sell Glamarosa instead because they do all that work for you, and it's exciting to open a box and not know what's inside."

"But they keep enough of your money for that surprise," Leo growled.

"The profit margins seemed great at first," Lexi confessed. "I buy the clothes for about fifty percent of what I sell them for. But then Glamarosa doesn't provide any of the infrastructure to run a business, so I have all the shipping costs, the racks, the hangers–"

"Endless amounts of hangers," Leo interrupted. "I buy them by the cartload at Costco. The looks I get."

"Right, all that stuff. But what really cuts into it are all the subscriptions. Glamarosa doesn't have an online shopping portal, so I use a service that someone else started to help us. And then I have to manage my own mailing list, and then there's the cost to enter the group sales, and my text service, and my live selling service, and the Facebook Ads..."

"And the returns," Leo said darkly.

"Returns?" Sadie asked, curious.

Lexi bit her lip and glanced around. No one seemed to be looking at them, though. "In the last six months, quality has gone down. Sometimes I'll get a box and half the items will be damaged. Bad sewing, see-through leggings, weird markings on the clothes. Glamarosa has a great return policy, they reimburse us, but..."

"But they haven't reimbursed us in three months. They owe us over $15,000."

"Me, babe. They owe *me* that money."

Leo looked down at Lexi, softening. "You're right. You're in charge. I'm just overprotective of you."

Sadie whistled through her teeth. "That's a lot of money. Are other retailers having the same quality issues, same reimbursement issues?" Amy had said her travel hadn't been reimbursed on time lately either, Sadie remembered.

"It's hard," Lexi admitted. "To talk about these things. Anytime I bring it up with my upline, it's kind of brushed aside. Just *trust* that you'll get the check. *Trust* that Glamarosa won't stiff you."

"Her mentor had the guts to ask her why she was so worried about money. That she needed to focus her energy on bringing the opportunity to others and not worry so much about the money. Can you imagine?" Leo blustered.

"Sometimes...never mind. I don't want to say it." Lexi demurred.

"I'll say it," Leo said, glancing around before leaning in to Sadie. "It's like a cult."

That echoed the thoughts Sadie herself had earlier. But could a business be a cult? What was the definition of a cult, anyway? Her fingers itched to Google it on her phone, but service was still out. She glanced around. Maybe there was a set of Encyclopedia Brittanicas around here somewhere.

"Speaking of your mentor," she said. "Were you on Steffy's team? Team...Rainbow Unicorn or something?"

"Rainbow Shimmer," Lexi said, blushing slightly. "Steffy loved rainbows. You saw her hair, right? She was all about rainbows and glitter and silver and gold, but with a rock n roll twist. And yeah, we were! I didn't actually know Steffy that well, there's about ten tiers between her and my mentor."

"I wonder what will happen to her downline?" Sadie mused.

Lexi blinked at her. "I...I didn't think about that. You should ask Paul. He's from legal, he must know what the procedure would be in this case."

That was a good idea.

"Listen, you're not going to tell anyone what I said, right?" Lexi looked worried.

"Of course not. I saw you and Amy talking last night, and I think the two of you should chat about some of this stuff. She'll listen."

Lexi looked relieved, and Leo nodded at her. Sadie glanced around the room, which was starting to clear out. But not Paul. He was still at the now-closed window, frowning out of it. No one stood near him.

Perfect time for her next questioning.

* * *

"Paul?"

He startled, spinning around to look at Sadie where she stood next to him.

"Oh yes, Ms. Moose. How can I help you?" He looked back out the window, frowning.

"What do you think you'll find, staring out there like that?" Sadie peered out the window. All she saw was swiftly filling ski tracks and a gray sky. She wondered when this would finally let up.

"Jon Jr and I ski together," Paul said quietly. "I'm just wishing he would have asked me to go with him. You shouldn't ski without a buddy."

That was definitely true, even in-bounds at a resort. It was even more true in the backcountry.

"You know him well, then?"

Paul finally turned away from the window, collapsing onto the window seat. Sadie perched next to him.

"I do. We work together closely. But then, I've known the Valentines most of my life."

"Oh?"

"My father was the triplet's lawyer. I grew up with them."

"So you've been involved with Glamarosa from the start."

"Not quite," he frowned. "The business was started almost as an afterthought. Amalia was a sewer all her life, you know? She started making clothes and selling them to her friends. Rosalie was good at marketing, so she joined the business to help Amalia reach more people. When the business became overwhelming for the two of them, Glenn stepped in. Glenn wanted to work with men, so he brought on their husbands. They filed all the business paperwork and were already making millions a year when they finally asked me to join as head legal counsel, and it was none too soon."

"What did they call the business before Glenn joined?"

Paul glanced at her. "They called it Rosethreads. Glenn was the one that insisted they change the name."

"Has the business always been a multi-level marketing

company? It sounds like Amalia was selling direct for a long time."

Paul shifted, looking around the room before deciding to answer her. "That was Glenn's idea, too."

For a business touted as for women by women, it seemed like Glenn and husbands certainly had a lot to do with it.

"I appreciate you answering my questions," Sadie said. "I have one more, if I can ask it?"

"Sure. I can tell you're trying to figure this all out. I'm happy to help."

"What will happen to Steffy's downline? It must be worth a bundle."

Paul blanched and looked around shiftily. "I'll tell you," he said finally, "but you can't tell anyone you heard it from me." He glanced over his shoulder, and Sadie had the distinct impression that he was wishing he, too, was on skis, skiing away from the mess his employers had made.

Sadie mimed locking her lips and throwing away the key.

"It'll revert to Rosalie."

Sadie sat up straight. Rosalie. Who was on Steffy's enemies list. "But she's...a company owner?"

"She won't be allowed to keep it, of course. Unless she was to resign, then sign up as a seller, but that would cause all kinds of trouble, jumping to the head of the line, etcetera. No, she'll be able to sell it to another retailer, or gift it, whatever she wants."

"Why does it revert to her and not Amalia? If she was the original business owner?"

"For the first twenty sellers they signed up, they took turns taking them on and teaching them the business. Neither of them get bonus checks, but they're technically their upline if you look at the paperwork."

"So Rosalie could just gift tens of thousands of dollars worth of bonus checks to another retailer? Amy? Lexi? The McCoys? Kenna & Brett?"

Paul nodded slowly. "It's not the best system. I've been recommending we change the legal process, but the Valentines haven't been on board with it yet. The company has just grown so fast, it's hard to keep on top of everything."

"Well, Paul...it seems you've uncovered a pretty impressive motive for someone to kill Steffy. It doesn't seem like Rosalie would directly benefit, unless she sold it for cash, but the other retailers could be trying to curry favor with her in hopes of her giving it to them."

He grimaced. "If that's the case, then I think the McCoys are out. They haven't been currying favor with anyone lately."

Right. The incident.

"What happened, anyway?" Sadie asked.

"They were on a live sale and made racist comments. Talking about afros and the ghetto and doing accents...it was in incredibly poor taste. They could've apologized, but instead they doubled down and did another live sale where their antics were even worse. Glamarosa publicly sanctioned them. Sellers underneath them requested to be moved to other teams, which can only be done in extenuating circumstances, but we granted the requests."

"Did Steffy say something about it, publicly?"

Paul nodded. "Steffy called them out for it. The McCoys were on the phone screaming at Jon Jr that she should be punished for speaking out against them, that it was against our ethical code of conduct for sellers to talk badly about one another publicly, but the extenuating circumstances meant we decided not to censure her."

"So the McCoys were angry with Steffy and Jon Jr."

Paul shifted uneasily. He opened his mouth to say something else, but a voice at the door to the library stopped him.

"Paul?" Glenn stood there, frowning at the two of them sitting side by side, talking. "Could you come talk to the group? I know you had a few things to go over."

"Certainly," Paul said, standing hurriedly. He turned back to look at Sadie. "Be careful," he mouthed. And then Sadie was alone in the library. A shiver went down her spine. She checked the window. It wasn't locked, and she left it that way. Maybe Jon Jr would come back? Maybe his intent wasn't to get away, but to go somewhere, maybe to try to get a call out, and then come back? Why else would he run, unless he thought he was next?

A log popping in the fireplace made her jump, and she felt uneasy. She was alone, the one thing she wasn't supposed to be. She took one step out into the hallway, but burly arms grabbed her before she got any further. She opened her mouth to scream, but a hand clapped over her mouth. Terror surged through her.

She really should've stayed with her buddy.

Chapter Seventeen

Sadie was hustled bodily down the hallway, further away from the meeting room, from the kitchen, from where everyone else in the house was, until she was pushed into a small, dark room, the door slamming behind her.

The light flipped on and she was turned, the hand still over her mouth. Her eyes widened.

"Listen," Alex, the boom mic guy, said in a hushed voice. "I'm not going to hurt you. But I need to tell you something. Can I take my hand off your mouth?"

Sadie's eyes bounced around the room wildly. They were in a small meeting room, like what would be used for a breakout session. There was a table and a stack of chairs against one wall, a white board on the other. Nothing she could use for a weapon. And the door was closed. Would they hear her scream all the way down here? She snapped her eyes back to Alex. Finally, she nodded.

He snatched his hand away immediately and took a step back, leaning against the door as if to keep her in. Sadie hoped she didn't regret her decision.

"I'm sorry to grab you like that," Alex said. "I didn't know how else to talk to you."

"What do you need to tell me that's this important? And where's your buddy?"

"Adam and Sam are filming in the meeting room right now. I'm supposed to be on a smoke break."

Sadie wrinkled her nose at him. "So you know I know Adam is Adam and not Nick Walker?"

"Yeah, he told me."

Huh. "Okay, get to the point, sir."

Alex sighed heavily. "Listen, how long have you known him?"

"Since grad school. But we haven't talked in awhile."

"I've only known him a few years. I did some promo filming for his startup. He's always been a nice, but intense, guy. But since he became interested in this Glamarosa project...he's like a man possessed."

"He's always been an intense dude. You know he took custody of his teenage sister when he was only twenty? That has a way of aging a guy, I think. When we were all partying, he was home helping her with homework, working two jobs to save to put her through college."

Alex looked grim. "So you knew his sister Ivy?"

"I met her once or twice. She must be in her mid-twenties by now. Do you know her?"

"I don't. I never met her, not before..."

"Before what?" Sadie's gaze sharpened on him.

"She died, about a year ago."

Sadie gasped. She clapped a hand over her mouth, her stomach suddenly rolling. How terrible. Such youth, such promise, wasted. "What happened?"

"She was struggling. She was depressed, and she...was in a car accident. It might've been purely an accident, or it could have been on purpose. I'm not sure. It was horrible. Poor Adam, man. I've never seen him like that."

"How terrible for him. She was his only family left."

Sadie collapsed into one of the chairs in the room. Why hadn't Adam told her? Hadn't she asked about his sister? She tried to think through the conversation they'd had. Had she asked? Had he answered? Of course, it made sense he wouldn't want to mention it to her. It had to be so painful.

"Shortly after it happened, Adam became obsessed with this Glamarosa story. He's taken a leave of absence from his business. He spends all of his time on this."

"If you're so concerned, why did you come to him with this idea?"

"Man, I didn't. He came to me. But I was worried if I didn't go along with him, he'd get himself in deep trouble. I thought I could help him, help protect him."

"You're a good friend." Sadie smiled at him sadly. A better friend than Sadie was. She'd been nothing but suspicious of Adam the entire time they'd been there together. No wonder he seemed different from who she remembered. He'd suffered a terrible tragedy, and it sounded like his life was upended because of it.

Alex shook his head. "I'm not sure I am. I don't know what we're really doing anymore. Filming in the hallway last night, that confrontation between Steffy and Kenna? Then trying to get film of Steffy's dead body...it's too much for me. But Adam feels like we're on the edge of being able to bring them down."

Sadie frowned. "For what, exactly? The business model isn't the best, it benefits the company owners more than the sellers, and the bonus check model seems a bit scammy to me, and I've heard they're a little behind on their bills, but what does he think the big scam is?"

Alex shrugged helplessly. "I don't know. He keeps so much to himself. But...that's not all I needed to tell you."

Sadie straightened. "Out with it."

"He's lying to you. Last night, I saw him go in Steffy's room, and I heard them talking."

"Shit." Sadie's mind whirled.

"Exactly."

"What time? And you said *talking*, not yelling? That's good, right?"

"It was around three-fifteen. And yes, talking."

So after Amy had left her. And Adam had come to her room just after four, claiming he'd found her dead after he heard a noise in her room.

"Did you see him leave her room?"

"No," Alex said hoarsely. "The next thing I heard after that was the screaming in the hallway. I grabbed my camera and hustled Sam awake, and we went out to film."

"He came to my room just after four and told me he'd found her dead," Sadie whispered.

They stared at each other.

"Do you watch all the footage you capture?" Sadie asked suddenly.

Alex shrugged. "I'm usually taking it, not watching it. Later, when we have everything we need, we'll watch it all, organize it, start editing."

"I need to watch the footage from last night. There must be something I'm missing. At this point, *everyone* is a suspect. There's so many reasons people here could have benefited from Steffy being dead. And now this stuff with Adam..."

"Okay. I can get it to you. I'll get it up to your room, okay? Leave it unlocked."

"Thank you, Alex," Sadie said, standing. "I need to go think about all of this." She remembered the packet of witness statements shoved under her mattress. Now would be a good time to review them. "I'm going upstairs to my room for a bit, actually."

"Be careful, Sadie," Alex said grimly, moving away from the door. "I'll follow you at a distance until you're inside."

"You be careful, too," Sadie sighed. "We're all in for it up here."

* * *

Sadie looked at her bed longingly, but resisted the urge to snuggle in next to Flower and just sleep the rest of this nightmare away. She had friends to protect. Amy, whose leggings were used to strangle Steffy after she publicly grappled with her over them, who'd been in her room prior to her death. Adam, her friend from college who was hiding things from her, and on a mission. Gavin, a new friend that needed to spill what he knew sooner rather than later. Even Ms. Beatrice, who she was pretty sure didn't like her very much, but Sadie felt protective over, anyway.

Sighing, Sadie retrieved the manila envelope and sat down in the chair next to the window, where snow was still flying. She took out the stack of yellow notepad pages and started reading.

Thirty minutes later, she slid the pages back into the manila envelope and shoved it back under her mattress with agitation.

Nothing.

She'd learned absolutely fucking nothing new except lawyer Paul had handwriting like an architect, Amalia and Rosalie's scrawls were virtually identical, and nobody had fessed up to being the killer or the duo in the library last night. According to these statements, everyone had uneventful travel, had barely been rattled by the landslide, and had all gone to bed at a reasonable hour, sleeping soundly until they'd been awoken by Shayna's scream. *Liars.*

Shayna's statement said she went to Steffy's room so early because they were supposed to lead the yoga session together, and she wanted to check in with Steffy on their plans. That sounded fishy to Sadie, but if Shayna killed her, why would she then scream, awakening everyone? Better to sneak off and let someone else find her, right?

Adam's statement didn't mention that he'd talked to Steffy in her room, or that he'd found her.

The only honest statement she'd read had been Amy's. Amy had written exactly what she'd later told Sadie.

Sadie checked the time on her phone. Ugh. She'd better go help Gavin.

* * *

"You!" Gavin said reproachfully as she slunk into the room, glaring around the kitchen at the intense prep work he was doing. "Ms. B abandoned me to go clean, and I need to serve an Italian buffet in three hours!"

"Sorry, Chef," Sadie said placatingly. "Let me wash up and I'll join right in."

Freshly washed and aproned, Sadie fell into the easy rhythm of working in a kitchen. Gavin was a firm leader, bossing her about without apology, but Sadie appreciated being told what to do now and then. She had two excellent Assistant Bakers, Max and Sage, and had handed off the coffee kiosk management to her partner Kendall, but she was still often the one that had to tell others what to do. That was part of being the boss, but it didn't mean it didn't feel nice to be the one to be bossed every once in awhile.

While she chopped vegetables to Gavin's precise direction, she thought through everything that had happened so far.

Last night, in the library, she and Adam had overheard a

man and woman having a conversation about a plan that had been put into place to occur with the Joneses. Without them there, they had thought the McCoys would be able to help them. What had the plan been? Who had been having the conversation? Sadie had thought it was a couple due to the amorous noises she heard, but what couple would it have been? If it was an established couple, then maybe Kenna & Brett? Or maybe Steffy and Jon Jr? If it was a couple that was flying under the radar, maybe cheating...the possibilities were almost endless.

Then there'd been the strange business with the clothing giveaway, and the skirmish over those rose-patterned leggings. Sadie shivered, dumping her cutting board into the prep bin she'd been assigned and moving on to cutting zucchini into strips to be marinated. Amy and Steffy had fought in front of everyone. And then Steffy had been found with the same patterned leggings wrapped around her neck. Had someone been trying to set up Amy?

After Sadie had gone to bed, she'd heard an argument in the hallway and had found Steffy and Kenna yelling at each other about Steffy being in Brett & Kenna's room looking for something. Steffy had punched Brett and was being led away by Glenn. Glenn had said in his statement he took Steffy straight to her room and watched her walk in before going to his room for the night.

Between that point and when Adam had come to her room, Sadie knew there'd been a lot of activity in Steffy's room, which was across from Adam's. Amy had gone into Steffy's room from two-thirty to three. Alex had seen Adam go into Steffy's room and heard them talking at three-thirty. Just after four, Adam came to Sadie's room and told her he'd found her murdered after hearing a loud noise. When they'd gone to get Ms. Beatrice, they'd seen Shayna standing at her door, screaming. It had been 4:25 in the morning.

Gavin called her name sharply and Sadie looked up, startled. "Next the yellow squash, then pop the mushrooms," he said slowly, like he was talking to a child. Right. Sadie had finished the zucchini. She put them in a different prep bin, this one filled with a fragrant olive oil and vinegar marinade, and tackled the yellow squash.

In Steffy's planner, which was for unknown reasons in the box Sadie had received from Glamarosa that had been packed by Rosalie and Amalia and delivered by Ms. Beatrice, she'd seen that Steffy had been spending a lot of time with Jon Jr and Amalia lately. She'd found a list entitled Enemies of Glamarosa in the planner, and it had included Rosalie, the McCoys, Brett and Kenna, and the Joneses, who weren't present. There were no reasons for them being enemies listed. The planner also detailed the value of her huge downline, which according to Paul, would now be Rosalie's, available to the seller with the highest bid or gifted to whoever Rosalie wanted to honor. Of course, Amy had told her than having a downline was good for the checks, but was a lot of time-consuming responsibility, too. Maybe being given Steffy's downline wouldn't be the honor Sadie thought it would be. Maybe it would be a burden.

But why murder Steffy?

Revenge? What could Steffy have done?

A fit of passion? Had Jon Jr and her had a spat, and he murdered her, then fled?

For money? Unless someone had an express agreement with Rosalie, how would they know they would benefit from Steffy dying? Any of the sellers present could be suspects in this case. Or Rosalie, too, since she would also benefit from the sale.

To keep her quiet? What could she have known? Why did she make that list of enemies? Would someone murder her because she put them on that list?

What had Steffy been doing in Brett and Kenna's bedroom? What had she been looking for?

Sadie dumped the strips of yellow squash into the marinade and started in on the pile of mushrooms she needed to trim.

"What are you thinking about so hard over there, anyway?" Gavin asked. He was prepping chicken for scallopini across from her, his filet knife quickly cleaning and fileting the meat.

"Trying to solve this murder."

Gavin was quiet for a minute. "Remember yesterday? What I told you?"

Sadie thought back. "To watch my back. And what I said."

"And to not trust anyone in the pockets of Glamarosa."

"You're in the pockets of Glamarosa."

He scoffed. "I'm just cooking their food. They're not even on the hook for me at the end of this gig, I had them buy me a one-way ticket."

Sadie considered that. "What do you know that you're not telling me?"

He carefully put his knife down, then turned to wash his hands at the prep sink. "Let's go outside for a minute," he said pointedly, looking around the kitchen like someone could be standing anywhere, listening to them.

"Ohhhkay," Sadie put down her own knife and washed her hands before following him.

He walked a few steps away from the door, ducking under the back portico to stay out of the snow. Large icicles hung down from the eaves. He peered around. Then, apparently satisfied they were alone, he said, "I overheard the Valentines arguing the morning we all got here. Rosalie wants out of the business. Amalia wants to change the bonus plan and is upset about some new line they're launching. Glenn's trying to keep them from screaming at each other at all hours of the day."

Sadie considered that. "Okay...that gives me some context."

"But that's not the worst of it," he frowned.

Sadie waited a beat for him to continue.

"Steffy–" but he was interrupted by a sharp pop, followed by icicles raining down around them. He fell to the ground, suddenly silent.

Chapter Eighteen

Sadie screamed, falling to the ground and covering Gavin's body. Was that popping sound a gunshot? She remembered the small handgun that had been in Jon Jr's pocket. Was he shooting at them from somewhere nearby? Why would he do that?

"Gavin," she gasped, her breaths coming in and out fast. "Are you okay?" She shook him. No response. *Shit.* She looked around her. No more shots had rung out. Could she get them to the door and inside? She had to try. Why hadn't anyone run out when she screamed? Why wasn't anyone coming to help them?

Sadie got onto her hands and knees and patted Gavin down. She didn't see any blood, but he wasn't responding, either. "Gavin, you have to wake up so we can go inside!" He groaned, and her heart skipped a beat. At least he was alive! She needed to drag him into the house. Remembering a disaster exercise she'd once participated in for the local search and rescue, she positioned herself behind Gavin, grabbing him under the armpits, cradling his head against her chest. She scanned her surroundings, swirling white with almost zero visibility in the wind, and took a deep, steadying, breath. *You can do anything for thirty seconds.*

With great effort, she stood, hunched over, Gavin's torso coming up off the ground. And she pulled with all her might, inching him towards the door. When she finally reached it, red faced and out of breath, she braced him against her, scrabbled behind her to unlatch the door, and drug him inside. Pounding music filled the chalet. Before she closed the door, she glanced out one more time, her heart tripping when she saw the smear of blood leading inside.

* * *

Sadie didn't want to leave Gavin, but she had to go get help. She took one minute to check his pulse and again pat him down looking for the source of the blood, but didn't find one. Grunting in frustration, she took off towards the meeting room, where Katy Perry blasted. *These people. What was wrong with these people?*

Sadie stormed into the room, straight to the lectern, and unplugged the speakers. The music stopped suddenly, and everyone stilled, staring at her.

Don't freak out, Sadie. Don't freak out.

Too late.

"What is wrong with you people?" She screamed. "You!" She pointed at Jonathan. "Your son is missing! His girlfriend spent a lot of time with you, and she's dead, and you're just...dancing?"

Jonathan had the decency to look ashamed.

"And you!" Sadie whirled on the Bautistas. "You sure have a lot to say about this company, but you're in here, playing their stupid games!"

"Now Sadie–" Glenn started, hands up, but she was on a roll.

"Don't even give me that bullshit, Glenn. Every single one of you has a secret to hide and a reason to kill Steffy. You're all self-interested, scammy assholes, and I'm done with you."

Amy looked at her, her eyes full of tears, from across the room. Sadie realized then that the camera was full on her. Good thing she'd never signed that film release. Her mind went to the information Adam was hiding from her. She couldn't even meet his eyes. The fight went out of her then. She was wasting time with these people. All of it was a waste of time.

"You!" Sadie pointed at Leo. "Come with me. The rest of you, stay here, in this room."

Protests went up around them, but Sadie ignored them. Before she slammed the door behind her, she stuck her head back inside. "Gavin was shot. Stay in here."

The last thing Sadie saw before her and Leo rushed down the hall was Rosalie fainting.

Again.

* * *

Sadie heard footsteps behind her and realized Adam and his crew hadn't listened to her instructions. What was Adam playing at? They shouldn't be filming any of this.

Ms. Beatrice met them at the kitchen door, alarm in her face.

"What happened to Gavin?"

"I'll explain while Leo looks at him," Sadie promised, pushing Leo ahead of her.

"My God," Leo exclaimed as he caught sight of Gavin. He leaned down next to him, starting to check him over. "Tell us what happened, Sadie."

Sadie leaned against a counter, but she couldn't stay still. She started to pace, her hands moving with agitation. She frowned at the camera crew, but they filmed on.

"We stepped outside for some fresh air," she said. *A little white lie.* "We were talking under the back portico when I heard a sharp popping noise, and then Gavin collapsed! He wouldn't respond, though he groaned once. I didn't see anyone, so I drug him inside, but there's a trail of blood!" Sadie put a hand over her mouth to keep a sob inside. She saw black dots at the edge of her vision. *Not the time for that*, Sadie Moose. She abruptly stopped pacing and walked over to the sink, splashing cold water on her face and starting to do box breaths.

"Hmm..." Leo said. "I don't see any gunshot wounds, but he has a pretty big bump on his head? That's where the blood is seeping from."

"The icicles!" Sadie exclaimed, standing up straight, water dripping off her face. "After the loud popping noise, the icicles on the edge of the roof fell all around us. There were wicked big ones. Maybe that's what hit him?"

"So maybe you weren't shot at all, then, Sadie?" Ms. Beatrice said, frowning at her. "I didn't hear a shot."

"Who could hear anything over that ghastly dance party they're throwing in there?" Sadie retorted, drying her face with a clean towel. Her panic attack seemed averted, at least for now. She cast her gaze over the prep they'd been working on. She wasn't sure that chicken could be served now. Gavin would be pissed when he came too.

Which he decided to do, at that moment.

He groaned on the floor, then coughed. "Stop poking it, Doc," he slurred, pushing Leo's hand away from the back of his head. "Hurts when you do that."

"Easy there Chef," Leo said. "You've got a helluva goose egg back here, and probably a concussion. We need to get you to bed."

"What happened, Gavin?" Ms. Beatrice asked, and Sadie frowned at her. She'd just told her what happened. And where had she been, anyway? Maybe Sadie shouldn't have trusted her so much. But what on earth could her motivation to kill Steffy be, anyway?

"Heard a shot," Gavin said, his voice clearing slightly. "Then lights out. So I'm not shot then?"

Sadie gave Ms. Beatrice a vindicated look, and Ms. Beatrice frowned more powerfully at her.

"Not sure why you're so pleased, Ms. Moose," Ms. Beatrice sniffed. "That means we're all in even greater danger if there's a madman with a gun out there. And wasn't everyone in the meeting room except for you two? Who could've it been?"

Sadie thought about it. Had everyone been in that room? She'd yelled at Freddy. Had Amalia been there? It was hard to remember with everyone dressed so identically. She shook her head. "How about you, Ms. Beatrice? Where were you?"

Ms. Beatrice drew herself up to her respectable height. "The nerve, Ms. Moose. Really. I was cleaning the bathrooms, then came down into the kitchen and found Gavin."

"I saw her pass by the meeting room just before you came storming in, Sadie," Leo said then, sitting back on his heels and frowning at Gavin. His eyes fell upon the camera crew.

"Stop filming," he commanded, putting up his hand. "This man can't consent to being filmed in this state. You're all getting out of control."

Adam looked like he wanted to argue, but Alex put the camera down and backed away.

Sadie was studying Ms. Beatrice. "Fine. I needed to ask, okay? So maybe it was Jon Jr? Maybe he didn't really ski away." Sadie hadn't told any of them about the gun. Maybe she should?

But it would be better for her to check and see if it was there herself, before she told them about it.

"Could be," Leo said. "But the long and the short of it is that we need to get Gavin to a room. Have anything on this floor that doesn't require stairs, Ms. B?"

"Certainly," she said, glaring at Sadie and sweeping out of the room in the opposite direction of the rest of the house. "His room is this way, anyway. Private Chef's quarters."

"Think you can walk with help, Chef?"

Gavin muttered his assent, and Sadie and Leo helped him up, each of them supporting one arm over their shoulders, and they slowly limped towards his room. "The chicken," Gavin muttered, and Sadie soothed him.

"I'll figure it out."

"Too warm," he grunted, as Ms. Beatrice opened the door and Leo and Sadie helped him into bed.

"I'll toss it and come up with something else," Sadie promised. "These assholes can take what they get and not throw a fit."

Gavin choked out a pained laugh, and Ms. Beatrice gave an offended huff.

"I'm going to examine him more thoroughly," Leo said. "As of now he's officially my buddy."

Sadie eyed Ms. Beatrice. That meant she had a new one. A hostile one.

* * *

"You don't like me much, do you Ms. Beatrice?"

They were working together in the kitchen, having thrown away the chicken filets and cleaned up the salmonella-infused mess it had left behind. After surveying the fridge and the pantry, Sadie decided to make a big pot of pasta e fagioli soup. If she had time, she'd make a few loaves of bread and throw together a salad. That would be enough.

Ms. Beatrice frowned from where she was wrapping up the hotel pans of marinating veggies to be served another day. "Call me Ms. B. And I don't dislike you. I just think you are very nosy."

Well she was making some progress with her, if she could call her Ms. B. Sadie let out a laugh. "You know, in January I had someone spray paint 'nosy bitch' on one of my coffee kiosks after I asked too many questions about a murder. I made a t-shirt."

"Why would you be proud of being nosy? It's nothing to be proud of."

Sadie shrugged. "Guess who found the murderer? Me. Not the cops. Me. Being nosy has kept my friends and me out of trouble. And you know Sheriff Wise asked me to look into this."

Ms. B muttered something under her breath, but shrugged it off. "Tell me what to do so we can get this started, then go tend to 'those assholes' as you call them."

Sadie smothered a laugh, but gave Ms. B instructions on vegetable prep while Sadie got the rest of the ingredients from the pantry.

While she was chopping onions, Ms. B started to speak.

"I grew up on the wrong side of the Berlin Wall," she said quietly. Sadie turned her attention to her, but didn't say anything. "My Papa...he asked too many questions. He died. I barely knew him. We immigrated here after the wall came down, started a new life. I still try not to ask too many questions."

Right. Sadie forgot sometimes, too often, what an immense privilege it was that she could ask questions. That she had the color of skin, the education, the financial means, the zip code that meant she could ask a lot of questions without spending her privilege. She swallowed hard.

"Lemme guess," Sadie said. "Wake up early. Want it more than anyone else. You have no one to blame but yourself for your failures. Hustle. Grind."

"As if there's nothing standing between anyone and their dreams except a failure to work," Ms. B scoffed. "You think my dream was to run this chalet?"

"What was your dream, Ms. B?"

The woman cast her eyes to the growing pile of onions, her eyes watering. "I wanted a family," she said softly. "More than anything."

Sadie wiped tears from her own eyes. "When all this is over, you come down to the bakery," she said. "At opening. Seven a.m. sharp. Any day of the week. I've got a group of ladies that would love to meet you." Sadie tried to imagine Ms. B sitting with her table of regulars. It gave her the shivers to think about it, which meant it was very right. Her table of regulars could inspire fear in the hearts of anyone in town with their vague, unobvious but glaring power, sharp tongues, and penchant for calling town officials in front of them to explain their behavior. They inspired fear in Sadie, too, but also love. That table of ladies had been with her since she took over, and were her biggest supporters, largest custom order customers, and loudest critics. Ms. B would fit right in.

"I'll do that," Ms. B said softly.

Sadie smiled at her. "These damn onions," she said then, briskly. "Let's get them in the pot so they stop making us cry."

* * *

After they'd gotten the soup on, Ms. B and Sadie went to check on the guests. Sadie hoped she'd let them stew long enough that

146

she'd open the door and they'd have sussed out the murderer for her. But when the door opened, she was met with the same sullen and angry faces.

She entered the room and stood, hands planted on her hips. All eyes were on her.

"Gavin and I heard a gunshot while we were outside, but thankfully he was not shot. A large icicle hit him on the back of the head and he has a concussion. Leo is tending to him."

"Oh thank God," Kenna breathed. "The back of the head is good. That man is too beautiful to have anything bad happen to his face."

"For the love, Kenna," Amy said, burying her head in her hands. "You are literally the worst."

"And you're nobody," Kenna retorted, her smile deadly.

"Ladies," Glenn snapped. "We're glad to hear that no one was shot," he said in a calmer voice. "I apologize that we didn't hear your struggle. I know you're new to our lifestyle, but in the Glamarosa world, we dance to lift our spirits. Even in times of strife, there's so much to be grateful for."

"Right." Sadie said it without inflection. She liked to dance as much as the next person. This dancing seemed like it was something else entirely. "We had to scrap Gavin's original dinner plan, but Ms. B and I are planning a simple soup and salad meal. I think it's a good idea for everyone to go to their rooms, or to their buddy's room, until dinner."

Sadie would go get the bread started, and while it rose...she had some sleuthing of her own to do.

Chapter Nineteen

Before Amy could slip away down the hall in Ms. B's wake, Sadie caught her, pulling her out of the stream of people escaping the meeting room and heading upstairs.

"I'm not like them," Amy protested. Her eyes were red. She'd been crying.

Sadie blew out a breath. "I know you're not, which is why I'm so confused why you're still a part of all this. Playing their games."

Amy's eyes watered again. "It's hard to explain."

"And I don't want to hear an explanation right now. There's too much going on. But I need you to have a real talk with Lexi. She told me a few things...I think you should compare notes."

"I will," Amy promised.

"How about now?" Sadie said as Lexi came up to them, a perplexed look on her face.

"If Leo's not here, who's my buddy?" She asked in a small voice.

"I am!" Amy said with forced cheer, pushing herself away

from the wall. "Let's go relax. Do you drink? I snuck a bottle of wine up to my room last night."

Lexi took her offered arm gratefully.

"I'll tell Leo where you are," Sadie promised. "Oh, and Amy?" Amy looked back at her. "Look again for the *thing* we were looking for earlier, okay?"

Amy looked confused, but then her face cleared. "Right. The thing. Will do." They disappeared up the stairs and Sadie realized she was, yet again, the one thing she wasn't supposed to be.

Alone.

Should she take advantage of it to snoop? The key to Steffy's room weighed heavy in her pocket. She had no desire to go into that room. And she really shouldn't disturb the crime scene. No. She'd save that for the absolute last resort.

What she needed to know was if Jon Jr had taken his gun with him or not. And she needed to watch that footage Alex had put into her room. Maybe that would give her enough information to figure out who the two people in the library had been last night. Then she could confront them on whatever their plot was. Would that lead her to Steffy's killer?

But what she needed to do first was get out of this hallway. Trying not to rush, she slipped back down the hall and into the warm glow of the kitchen. It smelled like yeast and cooking tomatoes. Delicious.

Ms. B was stirring the soup. The kitchen was spotless except for a big silver bowl with a towel over it. The woman was a marvel, really. It would've taken Sadie twice as long to clean up their mess and get bread dough started.

"You're amazing, Ms. B," Sadie said, peeking under the towel. The bread needed to rise for a bit.

"I figured you would have an agenda," she said, turning the soup down and putting the lid on just so it could vent.

"Always," Sadie said, laughing inside. Aside from being described as a nosy bitch, she was often accused of having an agenda. Of course she did. Those oft-satired signs well-meaning liberals put out on their lawns? The ones that said, "In this house we believe...Black Lives Matter, women's rights are human rights, no human is illegal, science is real, love is love, kindness is everything"...that was Sadie's agenda.

Ms. B took off her apron, throwing it in the bin for soiled ones, then turned to her, brushing her hands. "Where to first?"

* * *

First stop was Jon Jr's room.

Ms. B posted herself outside the door and Sadie slipped inside. The room felt smaller than the last time she'd been in it. Darker. Dimmer. Scarier. Like the walls were closing in on her. She hurried over to the closet and opened the door. Like Ms. B had said, the ski boots and clothes were gone, but his suit jacket was still hanging. She felt the pocket and her stomach dropped. It was empty. She quickly searched through the rest of the clothes in the closet, his empty suitcase, the dresser drawers, under the mattress. She looked in all the drawers in the bathroom, and in a particular moment of paranoia, even in the toilet tank. It wasn't there.

Jon Jr had taken the gun with him when he left. Right? That was the most logical solution?

But then he'd...shot at her and Gavin from outside? It made no sense. He should've been far away from the chalet by the time they'd gone outside. Why would he ski away, only to hide just out of sight? Was he maybe in some sort of trouble? But then...why shoot? Sadie's head hurt. There were just too many questions and not enough answers.

An owl hooted in the hallway and she realized she'd been in the room too long. Shit. She hustled over to the door.

"Clear to come out?"

"Took you long enough," Ms. B said under her breath, "but yes."

Sadie slipped out and Ms. B locked the door behind her.

"Now my room," Sadie said, going to her room and pushing it open.

"You didn't lock it?"

"I unlocked it earlier because someone was leaving me something up here."

"Who?"

Sadie scanned the room as they closed the door behind them. She spotted an iPad on her bureau "Aha. Alex, from the film crew. He left me the footage from last night in the great room."

"Sounds boring," Ms. B said, going over to the window and peering out. "It's starting to clear up out there," she said, her voice tinged in excitement.

"Ugh, I hope so," Sadie said, grabbing the iPad and collapsing on the bed, laying her head on Flower. She pushed the pile of Glamarosa to the side to make room, plastic bags falling onto the floor with a crinkle. She was exhausted. "I'm supposed to be in Mexico, you know."

"You've mentioned it," Ms. B said dryly. "What are you looking for in the video?"

Sadie entered the pin Alex had left on a Post-It and opened the photos app. The video was there, broken up into hour long segments. This would take forever.

"Last night I overheard a conversation in the library." Sadie deliberately left out Adam. "I'm hoping I can figure out who it was based on who wasn't in the room at the time." She thought about it. What time had that been? Eight-thirty? Nine? Sadie had gone up to her room just after ten.

She scrolled through the first video, watching the time-stamp, then switched to the second video. She saw herself join the group in the room and talk to Amy. The look on her face when Amy had told her she needed to change...yikes. She'd have to make sure to change into something nice for tonight's dinner. They got food, then sat and ate. She watched people filter in and out of the room, to and from the various sitting areas, back and forth to the buffet. It was all how she remembered it.

Then Adam walked up to her, and Sadie sharpened her gaze. This was it. She scanned forward until the two of them left the room, then paused it. She took in everyone's positions. Amy and Lexi sat on the couch chatting. Leo was standing with Jonathan, Freddy, Brett, and Jon Jr, talking and drinking amber-colored liquid from a rocks glass. Rosalie, Kenna, and the McCoys were sitting near the fireplace, heads together. Steffy and Amalia were talking near the buffet. Titus was sulking a chair near the window. Paul continued to eat cocktail shrimp and frown at the art. Sam and Alex were obviously out of frame, filming. Everyone was there.

She hit play again, scrubbing forward ten seconds at a time. There was some movement between the groups, but no one left the room. Surely this couldn't be yet another dead end?

"No luck?" Ms. B asked from the chair. She was studying her nails.

Sadie growled at the screen. Too much time had passed in the video. Who had it been?

Then, finally, she saw a woman slip out of the room. She couldn't see her face, but she recognized the pattern on her dress. Breath held, she watched as a man excused himself and stepped out of the room. No one watched him go.

Breathless, she scrubbed forward. After a good amount of time, they both slipped back into the room, one at a time. Then Sadie came back in. No one else had left, that entire time.

She knew who the amorous couple with a plot on the other side of the curtain had been.

Kenna. And Freddy, Rosalie's husband.

Ugh. Yuck.

Sadie hated cheaters. And here were two people stepping out on their partners. She needed to question them. Her mind whirled with possibilities of the plot they were up to. And in her head, she formed a plan. She would confront them, tonight, while they were caught in the act. Sadie put down the iPad.

"Figure it out?" Ms. B asked, standing as Sadie popped up off the bed.

"Yep," Sadie said. "Let's go make some bread, and I'll think about what this means."

Ms. B didn't ask any questions. She was really a great sidekick, even if she insisted on hooting like an owl.

* * *

They checked in on Gavin, who was grumpy and ready to get out of bed, which Sadie thought was a good sign. When she'd had a concussion last fall after being knocked on the head and left for dead in a garage with a running car, she hadn't wanted to get out of bed for days. And she hadn't, recuperating in a hospital while a killer ran loose.

Leo was holding strong against Gavin's insistence and was glad to hear Lexi was with Amy.

Ms. B and Sadie worked on rounds of bread, and when they were left to rise for a second time, Sadie told Ms. B she needed to sneak off for a bit.

Ms. B raised an eyebrow at her. "Buddy system, remember?"

"Right, right. I'll be careful. Everyone's in their rooms, anyway. I'll just be in the dining room, setting the table."

"For our buffet soup and salad?"

Sadie shrugged. "Fancy people like fancy things. I'll make it look nice."

"Check under the side table for linens and things."

"Place cards?"

"You are fancy. Yes, in one of the drawers."

"Perf."

"Be back in here by six, the sheriff's going to check in then."

Sadie snuck into the dining room, then pulled the double doors behind her and locked them for good measure. See. Safe and sound. She worried for a moment for Ms. B, but then remembered she was chopping salad ingredients with a knife as long as Sadie's arm. She needn't be worried about her.

Sadie made swift work of setting the long table. No table-cloth, one because she couldn't wrestle it onto the table by herself, and two because this was a rustic meal. She set out pale blue placemats, crisp white napkins, and the heavy hammered silverware. The divots reminded her of the pebbly skin of a rainbow trout. She set the bowls out on the sideboard buffet, ready for soup to be ladled into them later.

Then she rummaged in the drawer for the promised place cards. She bit her lip and stared at the table. She needed to be precise with this. She wrote everyone's names out in the nice handwriting she used to write the bakery's daily specials. She shuffled them around a few times, then nodded. If everything went the way she wanted it to, this configuration would have the best effect.

Now for the next step.

For this, she needed to go back up to her room. She didn't

want to disturb Ms. B. Surely it would be okay for her to just run upstairs real quick. At this point, all signs led to the killer being Jon Jr. Why else would he have bolted? And him and his gun were not in the house. So, they were all most likely safe, just sulking around in pairs just in case. And this step was important. She'd be fast.

Chapter Twenty

Upstairs, Sadie locked the door behind her, then quickly glanced under the bed, in the closet, and in the bathroom to make sure she was truly alone. She wasn't sure who she thought might be lurking there, but she couldn't relax until she did it.

Then she rifled around in her travel backpack for a notepad and pen and retrieved the witness statements from under the mattress. She sat on the bed and chewed on the end of the pen, thinking through her next move.

She scanned through the statements until she found Freddy's and Kenna's. She laid them out in front of her and studied the handwriting.

It took a few tries, but she was able to do a reasonable fake of Freddy's almost unreadable scrawl and Kenna's bold cursive. It would do, at least.

She put the statements back into the manila envelope and shoved them back under the bed.

There was something about the planner she wanted to check, but she didn't have time now. It was almost time for guests to start filtering downstairs for pre-dinner drinks, presuming they wouldn't give up that ritual if they hadn't given up their dance parties in the face of death and a killer in their midst, which meant she needed to facilitate the delivery of these notes before then.

First, she listened at Brett and Kenna's door. She heard a loud snore, which she presumed was probably Brett. Convenient. She listened for Kenna, realizing after a moment she also heard the loud drone of a hair dryer. Perfect. She slipped the first note under the door, giving it a good push, and hoped Kenna would find it before Brett did. This wasn't an exact science.

Then she crept upstairs to Freddy and Rosalie's room.

As she was leaning down to shove the note under their door, it opened, and Freddy stared down at her.

Shit.

"What are you doing?" He asked.

Sadie stood. "Uh..." *C'mon Sadie. Be a smart sleuth.* "I found this in the hallway and it has your name on it. Thought I would just slide it under your door."

He looked at the folded piece of paper in her hand like she was holding a snake. She held it out to him. He hesitated, then took it from her. She smiled at him. "Glad that worked out. Dinner will be soon, the soup smells delicious."

Then she turned and waltzed down the hall like she had a reason to be there.

"Hey!" He called out behind her, and she froze. She looked over her shoulder, ready to bolt.

"Where's your buddy?"

Sadie forced a smile. "Ms. B is down in the kitchen, but I'll be okay getting back down there."

"Watch your back," he said, then shut the door. Sadie felt a chill go up her spine. Were those words of caution? Or a warning?

As she neared the end of the hallway, her pocket buzzed, startling her. What? Were the phones working again? Or, more likely, she was getting a random push notification. Probably from Candy Crush, which she hadn't played in years but still got notifications for. Or, even worse, it could be the increasingly threatening Duolingo Owl telling her it was time to work on her Spanish. She ducked into the third floor sitting area and pulled it out of her pocket.

She had one bar of service. She glanced around. How was that possible? Maybe it really was clearing up outside and she could just get a glimmer of a signal in this part of the house. Excitement raced through her, replacing the chill she'd felt earlier. And not just excitement for news of the outside world—because honestly, the news was usually awful—but because she could get a call out. She bit her lip, wondering who she should try. They would be talking to the sheriff soon, so no need to call law enforcement.

She laughed to herself. Why was she even questioning this? She should call the one person in her life that always knew everything about everything, even when it seemed impossible for her to do so.

Kendall Craig.

Sadie selected her from her favorites and put the phone to her ear.

After two rings, Kendall's voice boomed from the speaker. "Moose! They finally got you out?"

Relief filled Sadie. Normalcy. There it was, just on the other end of the line. Sadie could hear that Kendall was out, where other people were. Maybe in a restaurant? She heard the clink of glasses. Ah. Maybe a bar?

"Not yet," Sadie hissed.

"Speak up, babe," Kendall said. "I can't hear you in here.

Nash is tapping a keg of experimental spring beer and we're all pretty stoked for it."

"I can't," Sadie said a little louder. "Go outside so I can talk to you."

Kendall must have caught the tone of Sadie's voice, because she heard her excusing herself, then the background quieted as she must have stepped outside.

"What have you gotten yourself into this time, Moose?"

"You seriously don't know?" Sadie was shocked. When was the last time she was able to deliver news to Kendall? It always went the other way around.

"I was up at the resort all day. Idiot tourists with Ikon passes kept skiing out of bounds in this storm and I spent the whole ski patrol shift playing find-the-Texans-skiing-in-jeans."

Sadie laughed despite herself, then sobered. "Okay, well I'm stuck up here, and there was a murder!"

Kendall let out a bark of laughter. "Of course there was. You know, Sadie, eventually they're going to start thinking you're the murderous one. Life isn't some Agatha Christie novel."

"I'm not joking, Kendall. One of the Glamarosa sellers was murdered, there's a dude here I know from college that's pretending to film a documentary on them but he's actually trying to expose them as scammers and also he's hiding a dark past from me, I was shot at today, my friend Amy's leggings might have been the murder weapon–"

"Okay, sis," Kendall said soothingly. "I'm all ears now. What do you need from me?"

Sadie wracked her brain. What did she need from Kendall? Why had she even called her? Just to hear her friend's voice, just to let someone know she was okay? Finally, she made a decision.

"Let my Dad know I'm okay, for one. And hug Tyrone for

me. And Kamari, too, though she'll pretend she doesn't want one."

"She's supposed to meet me here with Tyrone in about ten minutes and we're going to sit on the patio and get drunk enough he has to navigate us home, so done and done."

"Wait, my dad or Tyrone?"

Sadie could hear Kendall's smile. "Arlo said he might drop by, too."

"The Wi-Fi is out here and this is the first signal I've gotten. I can't get a browser window to work, but can you do one thing for me?"

"Sure." But Kendall's' voice was fading out, static overtaking it. *No, not yet!*

Sadie got up from the oversized lounge chair she'd collapsed into and wandered around the room.

"Kendall?"

"–breaking up–"

Sadie went further into the room. There was a set of bookcases along the back wall. Maybe if she climbed them? There was a high skylight above, is that where the glimpse of signal was coming from?

Sadie stepped up onto the first level of the bookcase, and Kendall's voice came through clearly again.

Clinging to the bookcase, Sadie described what she needed from Kendall. Find the episode of Next Fashion Star Steffy Austin had been on and save the clip. Why had Amalia been so upset Steffy had mentioned it to her and Glenn? Sadie remembered the grip Amalia had on her wine glass. Maybe the clip would tell her something.

"I'm on it," Kendall promised. "I won't even get wasted."

"Okay. Call and leave me a voicemail describing it and try to get a text through too. Or I'll call you back after dinner."

They were about to hang up when Sadie thought of something else. "Oh! Did you hear of any skiers coming down out of up here?"

"From your direction?" Kendall whistled. "No. That'd be quite a ski."

"The founder's son skied out of here today. We reported it to the sheriff, but I didn't know if you'd gotten any info through the ski patrol grapevine..."

"Search and rescue has basically been paged out for twenty-four hours straight. I'll ask around."

"Thank you friend," Sadie said. Her eyes got misty. She wanted out of this place. Yesterday all she'd wanted was to be away from Jackson, and now she'd give anything to be back home.

"Anything for you, Moose," Kendall was saying. She heard Kamari call out to her from a distance, heard a happy bark. She was about to give in and ask to talk to her dog when she saw something on the reflection of the vase on the bookcase in front of her. Something shiny, that was moving. She blinked at it, then screamed.

* * *

Her phone dropped to the carpeted floor as she whirled to confront the reflection she'd seen.

"Moose? Moose?" She heard Kendall's panicked voice through the speaker like she was under water, a distant sound from a world far away.

All her focus was on the barrel of the gun pointed in her direction.

The person holding it was in the shadows. The sun had set outside, the skylight no longer providing light. The little light in the room seemed to reflect off the barrel of that small pistol. It looked like the one she'd seen in Jon Jr's room.

Sadie squinted at the figure. Was it a man? A woman? It really was dark in here. Why hadn't she turned on a lamp?

Sadie put her hands up, slowly. "Please," she said softly. "Please don't hurt me."

The figure stood, unwavering. Sadie saw then that they wore some sort of covering over their face, over their head, and a big bulky coat. They were taller than Sadie, but that wasn't saying much. Most people over the age of thirteen were.

"Stop. Poking. Around." The words were spoken in a high, nasally voice. One she couldn't pinpoint, and she guessed was put on for show. It could've been a man putting on a falsetto, or a woman doing the same. Damn.

"Okay," Sadie said. "I'll go to my room and not come out. Just don't hurt me. Or anyone else here."

The gun wavered just a bit at that, and she thought she saw the figure's shoulders shake. Almost...like they were laughing?

"But some of them deserve to be hurt."

Sadie heard footsteps pounding down the hallway. Finally. Hadn't it been minutes since she'd screamed? Or had it only been a few seconds? Sadie wanted to yell out for them to stop, for them to protect themselves, but she was scared. And she needn't have worried. The figure heard the footsteps too and whirled away, the big coat twirling as they did. They disappeared down the steps and Sadie stood, wooden, as Glenn came rushing around the corner from the direction of his room.

He took one look at her and his face was grim. "This is why we're supposed to be on the buddy system," he sighed.

Sadie picked her phone up off the floor. The call had dropped, the signal disappeared. They were on their own again.

Chapter Twenty-One

Once again, they all gathered in the great room. Glenn pulled Sadie along like a puppy from room to room as he banged on doors and collected people to come with him. Sadie tried to peek in everyone's rooms to see if there was a black coat piled up anywhere, but she didn't see one, of course. She worried for Kendall, who she knew had heard her scream. She must be scared for her. And Kendall was rarely scared.

That's what Sadie saw in the faces of the people that traipsed alongside them on their way to the great room, too. Fear.

It'd been just over twelve hours since they'd been awoken to screams and a dead body. One of them was missing. Another had been shot at and had a concussion. And now, Sadie had been threatened by someone with a gun.

Someone. Sadie thought through again what she could remember about the person. Taller than her. Covered up in a big black coat and something black covering their face, like a ski mask except it covered everything. Spoke in a high, nasally voice so they wouldn't be detected. Really, how had she not gotten anything else?

Once Glenn had everyone in the great room, he pulled Sadie back to the kitchen to get Ms. B. She was on the satellite phone, looking annoyed, but when she saw Sadie's face it switched to concerned.

She put the phone down.

"The sheriff hasn't called like he promised, so I was trying to call him. What happened to you?"

"Ms. Moose was alone in the third floor sitting area and was confronted by a figure in black with a gun," Glenn said succinctly. "Please come into the great room, so we can talk about it?"

"Certainly," Ms. B said. "I'll see if Gavin's up for moving as well."

But Glenn wouldn't let her out of his sight, so they all went down the corridor to the chef's quarters. Leo had locked the door, and when he opened it he looked at them warily. Gavin was frowning at them from the bed.

Glenn filled them in on the situation, and Gavin insisted he could walk that far. Leo agreed it was probably okay, so with Gavin leaning on Leo, they walked again through the kitchen— Gavin had the decency to comment that the soup smelled amazing, at least—and then into the great room.

They were twenty now. Yesterday they had been twenty-two.

Surely they had to get out of this nightmare soon.

With everyone together, Glenn again repeated Sadie's story. All eyes were, once again, on her.

"It's interesting," Kenna said after a beat of silence when he was done, "that you're the only one who's seen or heard a gun today."

"I definitely heard a shot earlier," Gavin said firmly, and Sadie gave him a grateful look for the support.

Amy rose and came over to pull Sadie into a hug, and Sadie collapsed into it. "How scary," Amy said, rubbing her back. "I'm so sorry I brought you into all this." She helped her onto their regular couch and they sat together. Sadie was suddenly exhausted. She wasn't sure she'd be able to get up off this couch. But she felt all the eyes on her. One of these people was the person who'd just held a gun on her.

"Where was everyone?" She asked. "Twenty minutes ago?"

"Our room, together, of course," Kenna said boredly, and Brett nodded.

Everyone agreed they were with their buddy during that period, and Sadie sighed audibly. Either someone was covering for someone, it was Ms. B, which she sincerely doubted, or...it had been Jon Jr, having snuck back into the chalet. Sadie had left the window unlocked. Maybe that hadn't been so smart. He was the one with a gun, after all. But when Sadie thought about the figure, and about tall Jon Jr, she didn't think it was him. And besides, he'd skied away. Why would he come back here? How would he? It would be almost impossible to get back up the way he'd gone.

"Well," Ms. B said, clapping her hands together. "This is just a good reminder to continue the buddy system at all times. The sheriff missed his six o'clock check in with us, but I'm sure he'll call soon. In the meantime, drinks? Dinner will be served at seven in the dining room."

"I could use one," Jonathan muttered, and echoes of agreement rang out throughout the room. Sadie sighed. What else was there to do?

But then she remembered her plan. She'd almost forgotten her plan! She eyed her marks. Did they look nervous?

But now she needed someone else to come with her to

execute the plan. No way she was giving up the buddy system at this point. She glanced around the room.

She couldn't trust Adam.

Ms. B was busy hosting, and from how fast the first round of drinks was already going down, she bet she would be at it for awhile.

Gavin was...not in the best shape for sleuthing, having been helped into a reclining position on a chaise by Leo, who kept a watchful eye on him while he talked in a low voice to Lexi.

Sadie glanced at her watch. She needed to get into place, fast. Amy would have to do.

"I'd like to go upstairs and change," she said loudly. "Amy will come with me."

Amy startled. "Do you think that's a good–"

"I want out of these cooking clothes and into something cute. Please?"

"Just stay together," Glenn said. "Everyone else is here, so you should be fine." Really, was no one else considering the possibility of Jon Jr haunting the chalet? Did Glenn think she'd just made the whole thing up?

"Great," Sadie smiled, and stood and pulled Amy up with her, hustling her out the door.

They turned for the stairway, but instead of going up it, Sadie pulled her into the library. Once she closed the door behind her, Amy sighed heavily. "Do I even want to know?"

"You're a great sleuthing buddy," Sadie soothed her. "All you have to do is be quiet and sit next to me! That's it!"

She led her over to the window seat and pushed her into it.

"Stay here, I'll be right back," she said. Then she scurried over to the desk, setting up her phone to surreptitiously record. She hurried back over to the window seat and climbed into it, pulling the curtain across to hide them. "It's dusty back here," Amy complained, rubbing her nose.

"Tell me about it," Sadie said under her breath. "It's okay, we shouldn't have to be back here long," she said more audibly.

"Who are you expecting, anyway?"

But Sadie's answer was cut off by the sound of the library door opening, heavy footsteps walking towards the cold fireplace. Without the roar of a fire, it was almost too quiet in the room. Sadie felt herself holding her breath and forced herself to move it in and out regularly. She felt like she was being so loud! Amy caught her gaze and widened her eyes.

"Now what?" She mouthed.

"Wait," Sadie mouthed in reply.

After what seemed like endless minutes, the door opened again, and Sadie heard the sound of the door clicking shut and the lock turning.

"What did you want to meet me for?" An annoyed female voice asked.

"What? I thought you wanted to meet me!" The man said, confused.

There was silence, then hushed, panicked whispers.

Ah. Time for Sadie's grand entrance.

* * *

Sadie whipped the curtain open, and Freddy and Kenna sprung apart, whirling toward her.

"Actually," she said dryly, "I wanted you to meet here."

"Oh shit," Amy said, her eyes widening even more. Because Freddy and Kenna had been...embracing. "Gross," she complained, covering her eyes.

Sadie wasn't one to yuck anyone's yum, but it was a little gross. Freddy was old enough to be Kenna's father. And they were both married to other people. And also worked together. Okay, it was gross.

"What is the meaning of this?" Freddy blustered, running a hand over his comb-over.

Kenna looked cagey. She knew she was caught.

"Well, last night I was behind this curtain when you two were talking." Freddy's face drained of color. "And then later, Kenna was involved in an altercation with Steffy."

"A petty argument," Kenna said, faking a yawn. "Nothing to make a big deal about."

"Kenna accused Steffy of stealing something from her room."

"A mistake," Kenna insisted.

"And then this morning, Steffy was found dead. And it occurs to me, the two of you had a very good reason to want her dead."

"That's preposterous!" Freddy blustered.

Kenna looked thoughtful. "Tell me what I had to gain."

"But Kenna!" Freddy looked horrified.

"No, darling," she purred, stroking his arm. Ugh. Again, gross. "I want to understand what she thinks she knows."

Sadie rolled her eyes. Fine. She didn't know all the details, but she could surely bluster her way through this.

"Steffy knew about your plan. She was looking for evidence in your room last night, Kenna. If you killed her, the plan stays under wraps. Plus, there's the bonus of taking on her downline. Freddy could influence Rosalie to gift or sell it to you for less than it's worth. Maybe that would be enough to get Freddy to leave Rosalie finally and be with you."

Kenna smirked. "What is our plan, then?"

Right. She didn't know that part. To...overthrow the company? Why would they need buy in from someone else to do that? The Joneses or the McCoys? To start their own rival company, taking some of the top sellers and their downlines with them? Or, at least, to threaten that to get something within the structure changed? Sadie needed to either guess one of those three things, or get them talking more.

"Yesterday after Glenn's toast, you said that Glama sounded pretty good," Amy said suddenly. Kenna narrowed her eyes at her. "There're rumors Rosalie wants out. From listening to her talk, I didn't think she'd ever want to leave, so what could be pushing her that way? Maybe needing to separate herself from the company so you don't get any of it, Freddy?"

Freddy rubbed a hand over his face and collapsed in a chair.

"But if she does that, what will you have left? Kenna's business only. If she's not forced out once they find out what she's done."

"There's nothing in my contract that could let them force me out over this," Kenna hissed.

Amy shrugged. Sadie watched her in wonder. "Maybe not. So that's why you came up with a different plan. You're going to start your own rival company, and you're taking your downline and anyone else you can convince with you. The McCoys could use a fresh start. The Joneses, I bet, were on your list? They've had a lot to say about wanting to add products that Glamarosa doesn't have lately. An accessory line?"

Kenna sighed and sat next to Freddy. "It's a theory, you two, but you have no proof."

"So you kill Steffy, convince Rosalie to give you her downline, fake it a little while longer, and then you leave, start your own company, and you influence everyone in your combined downlines to come with. Probably give out bonuses, guaranteed leadership positions."

"It's a smart idea, actually," Kenna said. "But I didn't kill Steffy. Maybe if I would've thought that far ahead. I didn't like her poking around in our business. I was worried she'd tell the Valentines about my plan—she never knew about Freddy—

before I could fully implement it, but I wasn't worried enough to kill her. Nice try, though."

Freddy was red in the face. "Like Kenna said, you have no proof of this. We're leaving now." He stood and ushered Kenna to the door. They popped their heads out to check the coast was clear before leaving.

Amy sighed. "They're right. We don't have any proof."

Sadie smiled, hopping out of the window seat and walking over to the desk. "Welp," she said, checking her phone. "That's where you're wrong. You wouldn't happen to have that fancy little projector you used for your presentation so we can play this at dinner?"

Chapter Twenty-Two

It turned out Amy knew where the fancy little projector was, so after snagging that from the meeting room, they'd hurried upstairs so Sadie could change as promised.

They walked into the dining room right at seven o'clock. Amy had picked out a pair of flowy black slacks, a silky gem colored tank, and an open, lacy cardigan for her to wear, and Sadie felt like she should be boarding a cruise with a bunch of retired people, but at least, again, she was comfortable. Plenty of room to eat, and nothing to trip over in case she had to flee once everyone saw the dinner entertainment she'd brought.

The food was set up on the buffet table, a large soup tureen steaming with a crisp green salad prepared next to it. The bread was in baskets on the tables, along with dishes of butter and jam. Sadie's desserts for tonight had been meant for a fancy Italian buffet, so the mousse and tartlets were a little incongruent, but Sadie knew they'd be good, anyway. Everyone got their food and sat at the table, not arguing against the place cards she'd laid out, thankfully. They didn't even seem to notice that they'd been thoughtfully placed. When Sadie sat at the opposite end of the table from Glenn, who was at the head, she smiled at him. He quirked an eyebrow at her.

To Sadie's left were her suspects: Rosalie, Freddy, Kenna, Brett, Shayna, Julie, and, though it hurt her heart, Adam. To her right, those she was pretty sure were innocent: Amalia, Jonathan, Titus, Lexi, Leo, Alex, Sam, Paul, Ms. B, Gavin, and Amy. It was a little crowded on the right side, but no one tried to move. The camera crew had set up their equipment but joined them at the table. Hopefully, this would be their last meal together. The snow had officially stopped outside, a carpet of brilliant stars filling the clear sky and illuminating the piles of untouched snow outside. Sadie had checked before she left the library—she couldn't even see Jon Jr's tracks anymore. The sheriff never had checked in. Maybe the satellite phone wasn't working, or maybe he'd decided it would be better not to alert them when rescue was imminent, so they'd be caught in whatever their natural state was after the traumatic events of the last twenty-four hours.

Everyone dug into the food, and Sadie was satisfied by the murmurs of content from everyone. She gave Ms. B a smile. She let everyone eat for awhile. No use interrupting the meal they'd worked so hard on. But while everyone was distracted with their food, she discreetly set up the projector. It was no bigger than an auxiliary charger, ran on a battery, and hooked into her iPhone. She'd carried it in her pocket. Technology these days. Though she'd been glad it was so convenient. She wasn't sure where she'd fit anything bigger in her slacks.

When it was ready to go, she lifted her head and saw she'd caught the attention of the table. Freddy was mopping his sweaty brow, face red. Leo was eyeing him with concern. Adam looked alarmed, Alex amused. Kenna, as always, calculating. Rosalie, as always, oblivious. Glenn looked as if he was about to say something, but Sadie talked first.

"A little dinner entertainment," Sadie said with a smile. She felt bad that Rosalie and Brett would find out their partners were cheating like this. But it was the only opportunity she'd have to get a genuine reaction from everyone at the table if she did it with everyone together. She aimed the projector at the wall behind her suspects, so they'd have to crane around to watch. Just another way to put them on edge. Amy vibrated with energy on her right, on the non-suspect side of course.

With a flourish, she hit the play button. She cranked the audio.

It wasn't a great picture. The library fireplace was framed a little cock-eyed, only the bottom half of Mr. Chops visible, and it was shadowy and dim in the room. Sadie started it so they only had about fifteen seconds of an empty room before Freddy and Kenna entered.

She braced herself.

"I need to–" Freddy was half standing, but Rosalie stopped him.

"Sit."

On the video, Freddy and Kendra were discovering neither of them had written notes to one another. And then they were— ew—kissing.

Gasps filled the room.

Sadie heard a sob and realized it was coming from Brett. Her heart went out to him. But she kept her eyes on her line of suspects. She needed them to see their reaction to the next part.

Sadie and Amy's voices interrupted the lovers.

"What is the meaning–" Glenn sounded bewildered.

"Shut up, Glenn," Amalia spat.

"Everyone shut up!" Lexi screeched. Sadie didn't know the petite woman's voice went that high.

Everyone quieted, and the scene played out.

"There's nothing in my contract that could let them force me out over this," Kenna said on the screen.

Paul whistled through his teeth. "That's where she'd be wrong," he said under his breath.

Amy was detailing her guess on Kenna and Freddy's plan on the screen. At the words "rival company" the room exploded. Sadie watched her line of suspects carefully.

The McCoy sisters were red in the face, shooting angry looks at Kenna for being outed. Julie loudly denied they knew anything about a plot to join a rival company.

Rosalie was stone faced, with high color on her cheeks. Her hand still gripped Freddy's arm, her red nails digging into his skin.

Freddy was breathing heavy, his brow dripping with sweat. He was speaking in a low voice in Rosalie's ear, who wasn't responding.

Kenna was patting Brett's back, who was folded over the table, sobbing, his hair flopped into his bowl of soup. She stared daggers at Sadie.

Adam had his hand over his mouth, and he looked amused. *You're not the only one who can film, buddy.*

On the other side of the table, Amalia was whispering furiously in Glenn's ear, pointing at Kenna. Jonathan looked uncomfortable, shoving bread into his mouth as if to keep himself from talking. Titus was talking loudly with Lexi and Leo, gesturing largely as they pointed accusing fingers across the table. Alex and Sam had gotten up to staff the camera and boom mic, their dinner over. Ms. B was calmly sipping her soup. This had nothing to do with her. Amy had gotten up and gone around the table to comfort Brett, Kenna having abandoned him to whisper in Freddy's ear instead. Gavin was...trying to catch her attention.

"What?" She asked him. Glenn's voice was rising above

everyone else's, him and Amalia's whispered conversation spilling over into shouts with Freddy, Rosalie, and Kenna. He slipped into the chair Amy had vacated.

"Freddy and Rosalie arrived separately yesterday," he said just loud enough she could hear him. "I overheard Steffy talking on the phone, commenting on it. Then I heard her and Amalia talking. That's what I was going to tell you outside."

"What did Steffy and Amalia say?"

"Steffy was upset with Amalia about some product she'd received, really getting on her about it."

"I've heard quality's gone down."

"Yeah, but Amalia was...basically begging Steffy to be quiet about it. It was so weird. You would think she would have the power in this situation, right? Not Steffy?"

"Huh."

"Yeah, it was weird. So do you really think Kenna or Freddy killed Steffy?"

Sadie shrugged. "It's a theory. One of a few I have. But really I just wanted to see...this." She gestured down the table, where everyone was standing, shouting at one another. "What it would be like when they finally dropped the facade."

"I hope we get out of here soon."

"You and me both, buddy."

Glenn's voice finally cut through everyone else's. "That's enough! Everyone sit down and be quiet!"

It took a moment, but everyone finally did. Glenn took a deep breath, then looked at Sadie levelly. "I take it, Ms. Moose, that you showed us that because you have questions."

Sadie thought about it. "I do have questions, but mostly I thought y'all just deserved to know what was really happening. And, I think it's possible Freddy or Kenna killed Steffy because she knew about the plan."

Brett let out another sob.

"We didn't kill her!" Freddy shouted.

"I can understand how you would think that," Glenn said, gesturing at Freddy to shut it. "However, I can assure you, I already knew about Kenna's plan." Kenna's jaw dropped. "I did not know Freddy's part in it." His voice hardened. "I will be speaking to my brother-in-law about that. I hope you understand that there's a family matter portion of this that we'd rather not discuss."

Sadie shrugged. "Okay. But tell me more about knowing Kenna's plan. From the reactions at the table, that seems like a surprise to people here."

"Not me," Paul said. "We've been aware of Kenna's plot for six months. We've just been waiting for her to make a move we can sue her for."

Kenna's face soured. "For what, Paul?"

"There's strong non-compete clauses in your contracts. Which you would know, if you bothered to read them."

"You wouldn't sue me. You wouldn't want the bad press I'd dredge up. Wouldn't want me to expose what I know."

Paul shrugged and gestured at the cameras pointed at them. "At this point, we won't be able to escape the bad press. Now everyone will know what you were planning, you won't be able to do it, and the nasty part of the story is already out. We'll weather it."

"Did you know, Rosalie?" Sadie asked.

Rosalie swallowed hard. "My marriage is my business. But yes, I did know about Kenna's plan. I did not know...about Kenna bringing Freddy into the plan. Glenn, Amalia, and I are full partners in this business. Of course I knew."

"And Steffy knew?"

"She did," Glenn said. "I talked to her about it. That's one of the reasons I had her working with Titus to launch a new luxury line, as a defense in case Kenna did get her business off the ground. And she was keeping an ear to the ground for me, letting me know what consultants were thinking about jumping ship if Kenna did go live."

Sadie saw something on Amalia's face twitch then, and she wondered what it was. She sure had been quiet through all of this.

"I'm sitting right here, you know," Kenna seethed. Anger splotched her face red.

"Not for long," Glenn said coldly.

"Your contract is canceled. Immediately," Paul added.

Kenna sat back in her chair, arms across her chest, mouth pinched in a line. Sadie almost admired her composure.

"We didn't know anything about this," Shayna said pleadingly to Glenn.

Glenn frowned at her. "You're on probation. For this, and for the live sale. We should've done more when that happened. We invited you here to keep an eye on you both and hoped you'd be grateful, repentant, but instead you're both acting like petulant children."

Julie opened her mouth to protest, but Shayna elbowed her hard and she thought better of it. Probation meant they kept their business. They could handle that, it appeared.

"I don't believe Steffy was killed because of this plot," Glenn said. "Because it wasn't really a secret. Kenna may have thought it was. But in the end, she'll need to answer those questions to the sheriff whenever he finally arrives. Now. We've had quite enough of each other, I imagine?"

There were miserable nods around the table.

"I propose we take dessert to our rooms with our buddies, lock ourselves in, and await rescue. The snow has cleared. This should be over soon."

Sadie was almost disappointed. She wanted to know who had killed Steffy. She wanted to be the one to figure it out. But, she also didn't want to be threatened by a gun-toting figure in black, either. And she really wanted to be on the beach in Mexico. So she supposed she could hide in her room for the rest of her time here.

"Ms. B and Gavin, I insist on you leaving the dishes. It's more important for everyone to be safe. Will you two buddy up?"

Arrangements were made, with confusion arising briefly when Brett refused to go with Kenna, and Kenna staring after Freddy, who was being pulled swiftly up the stairs by Rosalie without a glance backwards. Eventually, Kenna was pulled in with the McCoys, although they were reluctant and looked for an okay from Glenn first, and Brett was roped in with the Bautistas. Ms. B looked longingly at the dinner debris, but seemed to agree it made the most sense to hole up, especially without any contact from the sheriff.

Amy grabbed dessert and a bottle of wine, and her and Sadie made their way up the stairs arm in arm. "My room or yours?" she asked.

"Mine," Sadie said. She was reluctant to return to the third floor, scene of her recent terror. Plus, she wanted to look in Steffy's planner again. Something was tickling her brain, and Sadie thought the answer might be there.

Chapter Twenty-Three

Back in Sadie's room, Amy collapsed into the chair by the window.

"That was wild," she moaned. She shoveled a spoon full of mousse into her mouth and moaned again, this time in pleasure.

"It was," Sadie agreed, sitting on her bed after retrieving the planner. She took a bite of the mousse herself. Yum. It was moan-worthy.

"But I don't think we're any closer to knowing Steffy's killer."

Sadie sighed. "You're right. Turns out Kenna's secret wasn't so secret after all." She flipped through the planner, looking for the list of consultants titled Follow Ups she'd seen earlier. She wanted to check the names and see if any of them sounded familiar.

"Do you think Rosalie could have done it?"

Sadie snapped her head up. "Why?"

"Well, if she wants out, could she have killed Steffy to sell the downline and take her money and run?"

"I'm sure they'd buy her out, right? If she wanted out?"

Amy grimaced. "What if they're having money trouble? I was talking to Lexi, and she told me about her damages not being paid back. Mine are behind too, now that I think about it. I've just been more worried about my travel expenses because of my credit card balance."

"They don't act like they're having money troubles." Sadie gestured at the chalet. "Plus Amalia is building that huge house. They flew here in a private jet. Hired Gavin."

Amy bit her lip. "Of course...but we all paid to be here."

"What?" Sadie dropped her spoon and stared at Amy. "I thought this was some sort of reward?"

"It is!"

"But you had to pay for it?"

"They covered the chalet, we just had to pay a fee for food and events. And our travel, of course."

"So not exactly all-expenses paid," Sadie dryly.

"It never is," Amy sighed. She stared off into the far distance.

Sadie studied her. "Are you okay, Amy? Financially? With all this?"

"I'm in too deep, honestly. And this weekend has made me think I should get out while I can. I like running a boutique, selling online. Maybe I could find a different supplier, one that doesn't require exclusivity. And I'd love to be free of my team. Everyone's great...but it's just so much work."

"Probably less drama."

"More work, in a way, but also less," Amy agreed. "I dunno. I always thought I'd do this forever. But seeing behind the curtain like this, I don't know if I want to be involved anymore. And if I didn't have to manage a downline, I'd probably be able to sell more."

"Well whatever you decide, I'll be there for you."

"Thanks Sadie. And thanks for trying to clear my name. I still can't believe whoever it was used my leggings!"

"Me either," Sadie groaned. "They must've been trying to frame you. And maybe me, too, by putting the planner in my box?"

Amy shrugged and yawned. "It's going to be a long night. I wish I had my phone. This stupid dress doesn't have pockets."

"Classic patriarchy. It's a business run by women for women and there are still no pockets."

"Well, Glenn's the CEO. And Titus is the designer. And Jon Jr is the VP of Retailer Relations. And the CFO is a dude. And Paul. Maybe we should say founded by women, sold by women, but it's not run by women."

"That's...very insightful, Amy. I wonder how Amalia feels about it? She started this business, right? She sure doesn't say much about it. All she's talked about since she's been here is her new house and Jon Jr."

"She likes to tell the story about how she founded the company, but she doesn't seem very involved anymore. When she started the business, it was simple, modular pieces. Like a capsule wardrobe, all the pieces could go together. It was a brand new concept, and she launched it right when people were talking about Marie Kondo-ing everything. It's gotten a lot more intricate over time. Now I want my customers to buy every-thing, not just enough."

"Huh."

Sadie found the list of retailers. Each line listed a number she guessed was an ID, a name under retailer, a name under sponsor, a short note about what they were struggling with, and notes about what Steffy had worked on with them. Many of the names were crossed out with a date and "contract canceled" or "quit" next to them. This was apparently the list of downline members Steffy had tried to coach to stay with the company.

When she'd scanned it earlier, she'd noticed one line that was different from the others. Instead of the normal notes about separation, that line had said "deceased".

Sadie ran her finger down the column until she found the note.

She read the consultant name.

And her heart stopped.

* * *

Amy insisted Sadie couldn't leave her room alone, but Sadie refused to put Amy in any danger.

"Stay in the room, lock up after me, and only open the door if I tell you the secret code."

"What's the secret code again?"

"The name of the bar where we celebrated your twenty-first birthday."

Amy made a face. "Makes me sick just thinking about it, but okay."

Sadie pocketed her phone and tucked the planner under her arm. "If I'm not back in ten minutes, go knock on the door of the Woodring suite on the other side of the stairs. That's Alex and Sam's room. Alex is a good guy and knows Adam is up to something."

"Are you sure you just can't wait?"

Sadie couldn't. She had to confront Adam. She couldn't believe that he was capable of murder. And if he had done it... maybe she could understand why, if her theory was correct. And maybe she'd see if she could help him. She knew a good lawyer.

The hallway was dim, the lights flickering slightly. She wondered about the generator that was running the house. How long could it run? She knew Ms. B had gone out to check the fuel at least once. She didn't want to be in this hallway if the power went out. She comforted herself remembering she had her phone, and it had a flashlight.

She stepped quietly in the hall, past the dark sitting area and the stairwell, then down to Adam's room. The key to Steffy's room weighed heavier in her pocket. She really hoped she'd have no reason to go inside.

Bracing herself, she scratched at the door, a quiet noise that would get hopefully only his attention. She heard footsteps inside, and a few minutes later, Adam opened the door a crack.

"Shit, Sadie," he said, opening the door wide enough to pull her in and close the door after her, throwing the deadbolt. "You're not supposed to be out in the halls right now."

"I know," Sadie said. She hadn't been in his room before. He didn't have much of a view. She moved over to the window and peered out at the dark night. No lights of rescuers coming up the mountain to get them, but she could see the lights of the valley far below. She thought of the cozy house she'd grown up in that she now owned with its apple-themed kitchen, ugly but comfortable leather couches, and backyard big enough for Tyrone to run. She wanted it more than anything right now, even a white sand Mexico beach.

She turned back to him and opened Steffy's planner to the list, holding it out to him.

"Why didn't you tell me about Ivy?"

He froze in the motion of reaching for the planner. His eyes met hers. Slowly, he stepped back, dropping to the edge of the bed.

Sadie stood firm, clasping the planner back to her chest if he wasn't going to take it.

"I'm so sorry, Adam. I'm so, so sorry."

He buried his head in his hands. "I should've told you."

Sadie softened a bit. She remembered him bowing out of

drinks after evening study sessions because he had to go home and help Ivy with her homework and make sure she ate dinner. They were orphans, with only each other.

And now he was alone.

She sat next to him on the bed, putting her arm around his shoulders as they shook. She comforted him, saying the nonsense words one said when they were trying to make someone feel better. After a time, he stilled, then wiped his eyes and sat back.

"She was so excited when she signed up with this company," he said quietly. "She called me, just bubbling over with excitement, couldn't stop talking about it. She'd been working in retail, and wanted to open her own boutique. I'd been talking to her about helping with her business plan, helping her get the financing, but I was so busy with my business, I just didn't get to it. I was cautious, I asked her about how the company worked... but nothing I said would stop her from joining. I just hoped it would be okay."

"She signed up under Steffy?"

He scoffed. "She kept telling me how lucky she was. She hadn't known anyone that sold it, so she'd gotten a random placement, and had ended up directly under the number six retailer in the company. 'Number six!' she would say, just full of awe. I hoped that meant she'd have a good mentor."

"And?"

"And Steffy Austin drained her of everything she had. Order more, always order more. It started with her onboarding. She talked her into buying twice as much as the minimum."

"Sixteen grand?" Sadie squeaked.

"Yes. Plus the starting costs. And then she needed to order constantly, always be recruiting, always be going live, always be selling. She was run ragged by it."

"I worry about Amy," Sadie confessed. "She always seems to

be working. She talks about the flexibility, but it seems like she's always working."

"Yeah," Adam said. His voice turned bitter. "That's the business model. Glamarosa makes money off selling to the consultants, and they promise they'll give business advice, help them reach their goals, help them build their businesses. But they don't do shit. They make them completely beholden to the company, then abandon them."

"And that's what happened to Ivy?"

"Ivy told me everything was going great. I believed her. I was so wrapped up in my own shit. By the time I knew things weren't going great...it was too late. She had a hundred thousand dollars worth of high interest credit card debt, and was swimming in product she couldn't move because it wasn't the best pattern, wasn't the newest style. Glamarosa owed her thousands of dollars in damages and missing product and wouldn't answer her calls. Steffy, her supposed mentor, only had the advice to keep buying the new releases. Ivy's mental health was...it was always a struggle, after mom and dad died. I didn't watch her closely enough. I should've–"

"You couldn't have known." Because now Sadie knew the end of the story. But Adam told her anyway.

"She drove off a bridge. Just like mom and dad did, except... it wasn't by accident."

"Oh Adam." Sadie wrapped her arms around him as he started shaking again, but he shook her off, standing now, pacing in front of her.

"When I was cleaning out her apartment, I found notes from Steffy. They were supposed to be encouraging, but it was all hustle culture boss babe bullshit. All about how the only person that could improve her circumstances was her, that she had the power to turn things around just by working harder. As if she wasn't already working too hard."

"So you started investigating the company."

"Yes! And what I found...Sadie, the Valentines? They're complete scammers. This isn't even their first multi-level marketing company. And Glenn? Glenn was involved in a pyramid scheme in the early 2000s! Rosalie wants out because she's made her money and knows the empire is falling. They owe ex-consultants hundreds of thousands of dollars. There are several states considering class action lawsuits. And yet they keep on hustling, keep on signing on new consultants, because they make their money on the orders."

Sadie swallowed hard as he continued to rant. When he took a breath, she said, "so you killed Steffy?"

He stopped in his tracks and turned to her.

"No," he said forcefully. "No. I went to talk to her. Alex heard me, didn't he? And told you? I should've just told you the truth from the beginning. I went to talk to her, and I asked her about a story I'd heard about Ivy Stroop, and she...was blank. She didn't even know her name. I left and came back to my room. I was in a rage. So yes, I went back over to confront her again. I didn't care about anything, about the fake documentary, about exposing them, I just wanted her to know what she'd done to my sweet sister." His voice broke.

"I might've killed her, Sadie."

Sadie stilled. As his chilling words settled in, the power went out.

Chapter Twenty-Four

A knock sounded on their door as startled screams rang out throughout the chalet. Sadie jumped. In the dark of the room, her breath was harsh.

"I might've killed her," he'd said.

"Sadie," Adam was in front of her then, framed by the moonlit window behind him. He got on his knees in front of her, his face in shadow but his eyes boring into hers. "I did not kill her. I was so angry. But when I went to her room, the door was open. And she was already dead. I checked to make sure she wasn't breathing, I promise, but she was still warm. Someone killed her in the minutes between when I left her room and when I went back. It wasn't me."

"But you admit you would have done it, had she not already been dead?"

The knock sounded again, more urgent. Hurried footsteps pounded above them.

"I don't believe I'm capable of murder," he said seriously. "I don't believe I would've actually done it. But I thought about it." His voice broke. "I thought about it, damnit."

"Adam, man, open the door!" Alex's voice, worried.

"If you hurt Sadie, I'll kill you myself!" Amy's voice, harsh.

"We can talk about it later," Sadie said finally. "For now, you should answer that door. Amy sounds pretty pissed."

Adam let them in, and Amy sighed in relief when she saw her. She looked at Adam suspiciously. "You said ten minutes, and it's been twenty, so I went to get Alex."

"I figured that out," Sadie said gently, hugging her. "Thank you. I'm safe, though. And Adam didn't kill Steffy."

"Well that makes four of us," Alex said. He held a flashlight in one hand and his camera under his arm. "Sam's refusing to leave the room and demanding hazard pay," he said to Adam.

"Fair," Adam said weakly. The fight seemed to have gone out of him after his confession.

"The generator must have finally run out of fuel?" Sadie guessed.

"Probably," Alex agreed.

"We should just stay here. Or in Sadie's room. It's bigger." Amy looked around, nose wrinkled.

"Yours is even bigger," Sadie mused.

"True."

Sadie went back over to the window. "But this room faces the direction rescuers will come from." She peered out. No lights headed their way, at least not yet. Maybe they wouldn't come until morning. Sadie knew quite a few people on the search and rescue squad. She didn't want them to risk their necks to save them if it wasn't safe. But she wanted out of here.

More hurried footsteps above them. Sadie hoped everyone was okay. Alex, Amy, and Adam were talking in hushed voices behind her, but she wasn't paying attention to them.

"All this investigating, and I'm no closer to the truth," she sighed. The voices behind her stopped. She felt a hand on her shoulder. It was Amy. She leaned into her friend.

"Well talk it out with us, then, *chica*," Alex said. "Let's hole up here and talk about it. What do we know?"

So the four of them settled themselves in Adam's cramped room, Amy and Sadie on the bed, Alex perched on the desk, and Adam in the only chair. Sadie went over what they knew.

It appeared Glamarosa was having financial difficulties.

Rosalie wanted out of the business. Her and her husband, Freddy, were estranged if not officially separated, and Freddy was having an affair with Kenna. Kenna was planning to start a rival company and take several consultants, including the McCoys, with them. Steffy knew about the plan and was trying to gather information for Glenn on what consultants were considering jumping ship. Kenna's plan was known to everyone with Glamarosa.

Steffy had snuck into Kenna and Brett's room the night before to try to find information, as far as they could tell, and was caught by Kenna and Brett. They chased her into the hallway and confronted her, and Steffy punched Brett. Glenn broke up the fight and took her to her room, dropping her off around one-fifteen a.m. according to his statement and Adam's recollection. Amy had visited her from two to two-thirty. Adam had visited her around three-thirty, then gone back to his room for half an hour before returning to find her dead.

Shayna McCoy found her officially.

After that, they knew so little.

Jon Jr acted distracted and jumpy during the morning session, and disappeared during lunch. Sadie told them about the gun.

"So it was him shooting at you and Gavin then?" Adam asked incredulously.

"I dunno," Sadie sighed. "Maybe? But why would he just hang around? And why shoot at us?"

"But then the gun made a reappearance upstairs before dinner," Alex said.

"I don't know for sure that it was *the gun*, it was just a gun."

"Let's say it was Jon Jr." Amy was working her hair into a French braid, her fingers flying as she talked. "If he killed her, he'd want to get away. He wouldn't have any reason to come back."

"Right."

"If he didn't kill her, why would he leave?"

They thought for a moment. "He thought he would be next?" Adam guessed.

"He went to go get help?" Alex proposed.

"Or maybe..." Sadie sat up straight. "Maybe he just wanted everyone to think he had left, but he hung around to prevent the killer from striking again?"

"How would he do that?"

"I have no idea, but when I saw the person in black upstairs...they said to stop poking around. It wasn't a threat. It was a request. They were imploring me." Hindsight helped her see the truth. She thought about Jon Jr's frame, his voice, and compared them to the person in the black coat. "I think it could've been him, if he was slouching on purpose."

They were all quiet for a moment, thinking that through.

A plan coalesced in Sadie's mind.

"If I was going to hide somewhere in this house, I know where I'd hide," she said finally. "Either with my mother...or in the one room in the house no one has been in since this morning."

Amy shivered. "No. Not in with Steffy!"

"That's why we'll check with his parents first."

* * *

They didn't like it, but eventually Sadie and Adam convinced Alex and Amy to stay behind. They needed someone to watch Steffy's door for...what they weren't sure, but it seemed like the right idea, and Adam's room was right across the hall.

So it was just the two of them that crept through the pitch black hallway to the dark stairway. The footsteps from earlier had quieted. Sadie wondered if people had consolidated rooms, or gone down to the great room to all be together. None of those seemed like good options to her. It was like the house was ticking around them, counting down to something bad happening. Or maybe that was just the grandfather clock in the third floor seating area as they passed by it, Sadie averting her eyes from where she'd stood just hours before, looking down the barrel of a gun.

They turned towards the Grand Teton suite at the end of the hallway and walked as quietly as they could, shoulder to shoulder. Adam held his phone flashlight out in front of him. When they reached the door, he glanced at her. She nodded, and he knocked.

She didn't have a plan.

She just knew she needed to know what happened here. For Amy. For Adam. For Ivy. For Steffy. Whether she was a nice person or not, a good mentor or a scammer, she hadn't deserved to die.

It took a moment, but they heard a voice on the other side of the door. Jonathan's.

"Who is it?" He asked gruffly.

"It's uh...Nick, and Sadie. We wanted to ask a couple questions."

Silence.

"About Jon Jr."

The door opened a crack.

Jonathan peered out at them, a cell phone flashlight on in his hand. "Amalia's not here. She's with her sister."

"Okay. Can we talk to you?"

Sadie thought he was going to shut the door in her face, but after a moment, he stepped back, letting them step inside, past him. He threw the deadbolt behind them, and Sadie felt Adam tense up beside her. This could've been a very, very bad idea. The room was lit with moonlight from a full wall of windows. This was the largest suite. From Sadie's earlier search, she knew there was a separate bedroom with a bathroom the size of her backyard and a vast living space. As they passed the bedroom door, Sadie wondered if anyone was behind it.

Jonathan sat in a chair next to the big windows and gestured for Adam and Sadie to sit across from him.

"Jon Jr's not here," he said as soon as they sat.

Sadie and Adam exchanged a glance. That definitely meant he was there, right?

"I don't know why he left, but he's not here. I thought Amalia might be hiding him, but I've turned this room over, he's not here."

"Why did you think Amalia would hide him?" Sadie asked.

"She's his mother. He's her only son. She loves him more than anything on earth, this company, our daughters, and me included."

"So you think he killed Steffy?"

Jonathan swallowed hard, then looked out the window. "I don't think he did. He liked that girl. He talked about a future with her. Amalia wasn't too keen–"

"I thought Amalia loved her?" Sadie interrupted. "I know they went to the spa together, traveled together?"

Jonathan's mouth was a thin line. "Steffy was...more into the relationship than Amalia was. She might've invited herself to that spa weekend. Amalia's gracious to a fault, but I don't think she wanted her there."

Sadie wondered why he was being so forthcoming with her. So she asked him.

"Why are you being so forthcoming with us?"

Jonathan cleared his throat.

"Something about this business isn't right."

Adam groaned. "Man, you're telling me."

"You mean Glamarosa, or you mean the murder?"

"Both, unfortunately. Amalia started this business on our kitchen table, staying up all night sewing. She wanted to buy clothes that all went together, to simplify her mom uniform as she called it, but she couldn't find anything, so she started making it. She didn't know anything about fashion. All she'd ever sewn was Halloween costumes for the kids and stuff for the house. But she watched all the seasons of that show, you know it, Fashion something?"

"Next Fashion Star?" Sadie said, suddenly remembering yesterday, Amalia's grip on her wine glass as Steffy talked about her time on the show.

"Yeah, that's it. She started selling clothes out of the back of her minivan to the moms in the school pick up line. She needed help, so Rosalie started helping out, got her on social media. It was Glenn's idea to turn it into direct sales. He has experience with business–"

Adam snorted, but Jonathan soldiered on.

"–and he thought it was the right way to go. Before we knew it, it was this huge operation. Giant warehouses on both coasts. Manufacturing overseas. Social media exploded this business for sellers, and I don't know that we were ready for the limelight. And then Titus joined the company and Amalia isn't designing anymore..."

"Did the style change?"

"It did. More trendy, more expensive. Amalia wanted this to be mom-friendly clothes for people on a budget. This new line Steffy was designing with Titus, it would have changed the business even more. Amalia's been upset about it, but Glenn and Rosalie think it's a good idea."

"What's Rosalie's deal?"

Jonathan puffed out his cheeks, but soldiered on. "I won't talk about family stuff, but Rosalie wants to be bought out. She thought it would be easy with the money that's coming in, but Glenn's putting her off, wants her to wait until the new line comes out."

"I don't want to be rude, Jonathan, but I've heard it's possible there are money problems. Some of the consultants are owed lots of money. And it doesn't look great, with you building that giant house..."

Jonathan held up his hands. "I have no part in the business. The house has been in the works for years. I don't know about the money stuff. But I do know that Rosalie hasn't been bought out yet."

"So being able to sell Steffy's downline would be a big windfall for her."

"Yeah, but nothing like being bought out."

"So you don't think it was Rosalie. You don't think it was Jon Jr. What about Glenn?"

"Glenn wouldn't do anything to hurt his bottom line. This business with Steffy...it's not going to be good once the news gets out. The media will eat us alive." He looked at Adam full on. "And you're not going to help."

"I'm not," Adam agreed, meeting Jonathan's gaze.

Jonathan sighed. "I don't know who it could be."

"Did you hear anything weird last night? Did Amalia ever leave the room?"

Sadie held her breath, wondering if she'd gone too far. But

Jonathan answered her question. "I don't believe Amalia left the room, but I use a C-PAP machine. I probably wouldn't have woken up if she left. But I can't think of a reason for Amalia to hurt Steffy. She's not capable of it."

Sadie looked at Adam. He shrugged. She couldn't think of any other questions. "Well, maybe we'll go ask Rosalie what she knows," she said, standing.

"Good luck," Jonathan said, ushering them out. "She's not one to talk."

When Adam and Sadie stood alone in the dark hall, Adam's flashlight the only light they could see, they looked at each other. "What do you think?" Sadie whispered.

"He could be blustering, but I dunno."

"Think we'll get anything out of Rosalie?"

"Doubt it, but we gotta try."

They shuffled down the hall, turning towards the stairwell and to the next hall that would lead to the mirrored suite Rosalie and Freddy occupied. They didn't make it.

Glenn was coming out of his room on the opposite side of the hall when they rounded the corner.

"You two," he said, his voice angry. "I've been looking for you both."

"Oh?" Sadie asked.

"I've been going door to door letting everyone know to stay in their rooms until morning, and meet in the great room at seven a.m. to wait it out together."

"Okay," Adam said. "We'll do that."

"But why were you up here, snooping around?"

"We...wanted to talk to you, actually," Adam said. "I was hoping I could get an interview with you. On camera. I have some questions."

"Now hardly seems like the time."

"Why not now? What else do you have to do?"

Glenn thought about it long and hard, at least in the shadowy view of his face Sadie could see.

"Fine," he said finally. "Fine."

"Really?" Adam asked, surprised. Glenn nodded. Adam looked at Sadie, who shrugged. She guessed they'd talk to Rosalie later.

"Okay. I'll go get Alex and Sam, and we'll film. We've got batteries for our lights."

Adam hustled Sadie down the hall and the stairway back towards his room.

Chapter Twenty-Five

As soon as they were back in the room, Sadie put a hand on Adam's arm. "Before you hustle out of here to interview Glenn, we need to talk. You heard Jonathan say Amalia used to watch Next Fashion Star, right?"

"Yeah. Oh wait. Yeah!" Adam's eyes were wide.

Alex and Amy huddled around them, confused.

"What were you saying about Steffy being on Next Fashion Star?" Alex asked. "I have a buddy that works on that show."

"She told me yesterday she was on it, just in the initial casting rounds, when Glenn and I were talking about Gavin, Amalia, and me all being on reality TV shows. Amalia seemed stressed when she overheard her, but it wasn't clear why."

"I actually have that clip," Adam said, walking over to rummage through a bag. He brought out his laptop. "It's about thirty seconds long, from what I remember."

"Why do you have it?" Amy asked suspiciously.

"I've been investigating all the top retailers," Adam admitted.

"Were you investigating me?"

"No," he said. "I remembered you as Sadie's friend. I didn't think you were doing anything wrong."

"Well that's something at least." Amy straightened her shoulders.

Adam queued up the clip. The three judges, a supermodel, designer, and magazine editor, sat at a table. A petite, mousy, brown-haired woman entered, rolling a rack of clothes with her. "Stefanie Crowley, 27, Seattle, WA" the chyron read.

"That's Steffy?" Amy said squinting at the laptop.

"Her married name," Adam said. "She changed it back to Austin when her divorce was finalized not long after."

Sadie shushed them both so she could hear. On the screen, the judges were asking Steffy about herself. She said she was an independent designer, and her idea was—

"Holy shit!" Amy exclaimed. "That's an Iris! And a Rose! And a Lilac!"

Adam paused the video on a close up of her clothing rack. Amy was screeching, pointing at the screen.

Sadie and Alex looked at each other.

"You're right, Amy!" Adam said excitedly. "I haven't seen this in months, not since we started filming and I got used to seeing these pieces every day."

"I can't believe this!"

"Can you explain to us, please?" Sadie asked, annoyed. She peered at the screen. She saw simple pieces, clean lines, but no flowers.

Amy took a deep breath. "That's Steffy, over five years ago, showing the pieces that Amalia debuted when the company was still Rosethreads. The Iris skirt you wore yesterday. The Rose cardigan. The Lilac tee. And I think an early Delphinium pant?"

Finally, Sadie got it. "You mean..."

"She means that this video makes it look like these pieces,

the idea of this capsule wardrobe of pieces that all go together, it was originally Steffy's idea."

"Not Amalia's," Amy said, her voice high, panicky.

"And if it wasn't Amalia's idea…"

"Steffy was blackmailing her," Adam whispered.

"That would explain why she always got the best product, the most product, the most random placement of retailers–"

"–like Ivy," Sadie whispered to Adam, and his jaw clenched. "Gavin told me he heard Steffy getting on Amalia's case yesterday before everyone else arrived, something about her being mad about product, about money."

"They acted like they hadn't seen each other in the great room," Amy said.

"It was all an act. That must have been why Steffy dropped that info about this clip into that conversation with Glenn yesterday. She wanted more money from Amalia, and was threatening to expose her."

"So Amalia killed her," Adam said, the words cold and final in the quiet room.

"Shit," Sadie said, shocked. "I think we figured it out."

A knock at the door, then Glenn's voice. "Are you ready yet?" He asked crankily.

"For what?" Amy asked.

"Glenn just agreed to go on camera and let me ask him any questions I want," Adam said uneasily.

"That's huge dude," Alex said, standing to gather his stuff.

"I don't think we should leave you guys right now, though."

"Should we tell Glenn what we know?"

"What if we tell him and he gets mad at Amalia and they fight or something? Or what if it causes some other trouble? It'd probably be better to just wait until the sheriff gets here, and then tell him then," Sadie reasoned. "Amy and I will stay in here, door closed. Promise."

Amy looked unsure, but she nodded. "Go ask Glenn questions. Sadie and I will stay here until you come back, locked in."

It was a bustle of activity, but within a few minutes, Sadie and Amy were alone in Adam's room.

They huddled on the bed together, whispering.

"I can't believe that Amalia stole the idea from Steffy," Amy kept saying.

"I can't believe Amalia killed her," Sadie kept saying.

A noise in the hallway drew both of their attention sharply to the door.

"What the fuck?" Amy whispered as they both hurried to it, peering out of the peephole.

"What?" Sadie hissed, shoving her aside so she could look out the peephole instead. She didn't see anything out of the ordinary.

"I swear to God someone just went in that room. I saw the door shut behind them."

"Ugh," Sadie groaned, leaning against the door. "We have to see who it is. What if they're destroying evidence?"

"I'm not going in there! There's a *dead body* in there, remember? And what if it's Amalia? We just decided she killed Steffy!"

Sadie knew all that. But she needed to know who had gone into that room. Both because she was curious, and it felt like it was her duty. The sheriff had asked her to keep her eye out. And here was someone perhaps messing with evidence.

"Okay," Sadie said. "I'm going over there. I'm taking my phone. I'm not going to get involved, but I'm going to get a picture of whoever's in there for the sheriff. And then I'm going to high tail it back over here and we're going to hide in here until the sheriff himself comes to get us."

"What if whoever it is comes after you?" Amy said, panicked.

"This door is sturdy. We'll put the chair under the handle. And we can hide in the bathroom, too."

"What if they shoot through the door?" Amy's voice had calmed a little. She'd always been better with a plan.

"Then everyone in the chalet will hear and come to our rescue while we cower in the bathtub?"

"Oof." Amy sighed. "Okay. You're right. You go. I'll stay here and watch and wait for you." She pulled her phone out of her pocket. "I'm armed."

Sadie gave her a hug. "You're a good friend, Amy."

"So are you, Sadie. Now go gather evidence and get your booty back here."

* * *

The door wasn't locked.

All day, Sadie had carried around that key in her pocket, insisting to Amy she had to wear something with pockets instead of the dress she'd tried to put her in at dinner so she could carry it. It'd weighed heavy all day, and she didn't even need it.

Holding her breath and phone in hand, camera open and video recording, Sadie turned the doorknob and pushed the door open wide enough she could see inside. She kept her eyes averted from the bed.

Her first thought was that it was freezing in the room.

Of course, Ms. B would have turned the heater off in here. For practical reasons and...more practical reasons. Sadie shuddered.

The room was still, though. Had Amy really seen someone? But why would the door be unlocked?

Sadie took a step into the room, and though she didn't want to, she shut the door quietly behind her. Wouldn't do to get caught in here by anyone else. Her breath was the only sound. She kept her phone up and recording in front of her. Man. Was she going to have to actually search? She was hoping for a quick pic, then bolting.

The figure on the bed loomed in her side vision. Why on earth would someone come in here?

She took one more step.

And heard the gun cock.

"Don't take another step," Amalia Valentine said from behind her.

Chapter Twenty-Six

"Turn your phone off."

Sadie took a shuddery breath.

She heard Amalia take a step closer to her.

"Phone. Off."

Sadie shakily turned her phone off, darkening the screen.

"Put it in your pocket."

Sadie did, slowly. Her fingers worked over it as she slipped it in. Had she turned it back on? For the love of Steve Jobs, don't fail me now, iPhone, she thought.

"Now walk over to the chair by the window and sit in it."

Sadie did, her steps quiet on the thick carpet. Her heart was racing. She wanted to scream for help, but Amy would come bursting through the door, and what would Amalia do? Shoot her? If she just complied, maybe Amy would go get help when she didn't immediately return instead of coming in. They hadn't gone over that part of the plan! Why hadn't they gone over that part of the plan?

Sadie sat in the chair, and when she did, she got her first glance at Amalia.

This was not the composed woman Sadie had met yesterday

afternoon. Her hair was scraped back into a messy bun. Her makeup was smudged around her wide eyes, which kept flitting around the room. To Steffy, on the bed, then back to Sadie, to the window, then back to Sadie. She held the gun in front of her, unwavering.

"Why?" Sadie asked after a beat of silence.

Amalia scoffed. "Why what? I didn't kill her." She jerked her head at the body in the bed.

Sadie blinked. "What the fuck? Then really, why? Why are you doing this? Why are you in here?"

"I told him to run," Amalia said in an almost-whisper. Her eyes filled with tears.

"Jon Jr? Jon killed her?"

"For me," Amalia whimpered. "Jonny found out about her blackmailing me. He found out she was trying to steal the company from me, sapping it of all of it's money. She was power grabbing. A heartless bitch. She couldn't have done what I did. She was going to crown herself the princess of the company I built from nothing."

Amalia swiped at her eyes with her free hand, the gun wavering slightly. Sadie held her breath again. One slip of her finger, and she was done for.

"This new line she was planning with Titus, the *designer* my darling brother insisted we hire, taking me out of the process. It was disgusting. Gaudy, flashy. Fabrics that would wrinkle during shipment. So much more work for sellers! They'd have to steam things when they got them, then they'd just wrinkle again when they sold them to their customers. No one ever thinks of those things but me, you know. I'm the one that started this business, and they don't even listen to me. They just pat my head. Especially her." She pulled a face at the bed. "She was always inviting herself along to things. Always reminding me about my one little mistake, always telling me I owed her more and more. She was going to run the company into the ground. We were getting behind on bills, having to take shortcuts with manufacturing, just to fulfill her needs. She always needed more."

Yikes. Sadie was starting to think maybe it hadn't been Jon Jr that had killed Steffy. "So Glenn knows about this?"

"My darling brother knows *nothing*," Amalia sneered. "He's oblivious to *everything*. I still maintain majority control of the business. I made the decisions that needed to be made to keep Steffy happy."

Huh. So Glenn hadn't been lying to her face about not knowing who would've wanted to kill Steffy.

"So...Jon killed her so she would stop blackmailing the business?"

Amalia's eyes snapped back at her from where they'd wandered away. "He finally saw her for who she was. She goaded him into it. She made him do it, by acting the way she acted. So I told him to run."

Ski, the sarcastic part of Sadie's brain that she could never turn off said.

"And now, I'll have to kill you," Amalia said nonchalantly. "To protect him. He's my only son, you know. I'll do anything to protect him. Including kill you, now that you know the truth. You nosy thing. You're not even supposed to be here."

There, she spoke the truth. Sadie didn't belong here, and hadn't from the first moment. She should've dropped her baked goods, hugged Amy, and ran.

Except.

Except she wouldn't have gotten to know Gavin. Or found out what was haunting Adam. Or make a new friend in Ms. B.

Sadie was trying to decide how to bargain for her life, praying Amy wouldn't come through the door while praying at the same time she would, when the bathroom door crashed open. Standing there was her salvation: Jon Jr.

* * *

Amalia swung around in shock. When she saw who was standing there, she let out a sob.

"Jonny! What are you doing here? I told you to run!"

Jon had his own gun, and as if in slow motion, Sadie saw him lift it, pointing it at his own mother.

"Mom. It's time to stop with the lies."

Sadie gulped. Suddenly, no one was looking at her. Should she try to get away? How? The only way out was right through the crossfire between mother and son. While she considered it, Jon started talking again.

"I want to help you, Mom. You've hurt so many people. I want to help you get help."

"I was just protecting you, Jonny. Protecting what I built for you. She was going to destroy it."

Jon crept closer to her. "I know Mom. I know, now, about... your little mistake. I think we could've worked it out differently, though. I loved Steffy." His voice broke, his eyes flickering to the bed, his face ashen in the moonlight. "I loved her."

"No, *I* love you. I was *protecting* you."

"Okay, Mom. You can explain it to me later. For now, would you please just put the gun down?"

Amalia seemed to realize she was holding a gun on her own beloved son for the first time. She started to shake, but then seemed to remember that Sadie was there.

"But her, Jonny! She knows!" She waved the gun in Sadie's direction, and Sadie ducked. She did not feel good about this.

"She seems reasonable. She won't say anything." Jon locked eyes with her, pleading. "Right Sadie?"

Sadie wasn't dumb. She could play along. "Absolutely. I won't say a word. Not to anyone."

"See, Mom? It's okay. Just please, put the gun down."

Amalia crumpled to the floor then, the gun bouncing on the carpet next to her. She sobbed, and Jon slipped his gun into his pocket, coming over to get the other gun and put the safety on before wrapping his mother in his arms. His eyes met Sadie's.

"Go get help," he mouthed. "Please."

Sadie didn't need to be told twice.

She met a wide-eyed Amy at the door, collapsing into her arms.

* * *

Sadie shakily locked Steffy's door behind her and bundled Amy back into Adam's room.

"It was Amalia. Or Jon Jr. One or the other of them killed Steffy," Sadie whimpered into Amy's arms. "We need to get Jon Jr help though. Amalia's hysterical. I think it was Amalia. God, I don't know."

"Okay," Amy said calmly, patting her back. "Okay. Should we tell Glenn?"

"I'm scared to tell Glenn, what if he does something stupid?"

"Leo!" Amy said. "He's a doctor, he should be able to help her, right?"

That sounded like as good of a plan as any. They made their way to the room, sneaking up to the third floor as quickly as they could. Leo answered the door when they scratched on it.

"Amalia's hysterical. I think she killed Steffy, who was blackmailing her for stealing her design ideas. Or maybe Jon Jr did it, but either way, Jon Jr asked me for help. They're...in Steffy's room. Here's the key."

To his credit, he just turned, got a bag from his room, and told them to show him the way. Lexi was asleep, apparently. "She already took two melatonin, she's out," he said when they both peeked in the room. "And Brett left awhile ago to talk to Kenna."

He was unlocking the door to Steffy's room when they heard the knocking. Leo took one look inside Steffy's room and turned back to them, grimacing. "I'll give her something to calm her down." They could hear Amalia sobbing. "You go."

They knocked on every door on the way downstairs, gathering pajama-d, terrified people along the way.

"Who could be knocking?"

"What's happening?"

"Where's Amalia?"

"What's going on?"

But Sadie and Amy just herded everyone along to the front entry. They interrupted Glenn's interview, Adam scowling at them, but Sadie insisting they needed to all gather. Gavin and Ms. B came through the hall to meet them, just as confused as they were. Wouldn't the sheriff have called to say he was coming? Why would he knock?

When they were gathered in the front entry, Glenn opened the door. Sadie couldn't see over everyone huddled together. She hung back, arm slung around Amy, quickly whispering to Gavin what had just happened.

But then all heads turned her way, and she stopped whispering.

Glenn sighed. "Sadie Moose? It's for you."

Chapter Twenty-Seven

S un.
Glorious, glorious sun.
Drinks.
Glorious, glorious drinks.
Sand.

Glorious—Sadie shifted in her chaise uncomfortably, brushing sand off her bottom before resettling. Maybe the sand wasn't that glorious, after all.

And true, she was under a beach umbrella. Her northern latitudes complexion couldn't handle the sun for long. But the drinks, they were flowing.

She'd finally made it to Cabo eight hours ago. She'd been in an exhausted haze as she was shown to her room and had fallen into bed after peeling off her travel clothes and slept for six hours. Now she relaxed on the beach, waves crashing nearby, and sipped her margarita while she waited for her plate of nachos to arrive.

The last seventy-two hours seemed like a bad dream.

The first half had been spent locked in the chalet, running from a broken woman who was trying to save what she created from another woman's ideas. Then had come the knock on the door.

Sadie had pushed her way to the front of the crowd, her eyes refusing to believe what she was seeing until she was close enough she could brush the snow off Kendall's jacket. Kamari stood next to her, grinning. They both held their helmets and had backpacks on, their skis discarded behind them. Sadie had stared at them in shock, speechless.

"Well," Kamari had drawled, "looks like she's okay after all, Kendall. Should we ski away? We earned these turns."

"I'm too hungry," Kendall had complained. "I was told a TV chef was here."

And then they'd heard the snowmobiles in the distance, approaching them.

Sadie's one phone call to Kendall had set off a chain reaction of events. Kendall had called the sheriff, demanding they investigate what she'd heard as the call had dropped. When the sheriff had said they'd tried and couldn't make it in the dark, Kendall had taken it into her own hands. Her and Kamari had hitched a ride up the nearby resort slopes in a groomer, then traversed the mountain on skis until they could ski down to the chalet. All for Sadie. To make sure she was okay.

She really did have the best friends in the world.

The search and rescue snowmobiles arrived soon after. Apparently Sheriff Wise had called Police Detective Nolan and told him about Kendall's call, and Detective Nolan had told him that he'd better get up there right away. That if Sadie was in trouble, there was something big going on, and they needed to get up there no matter what.

So Sadie guessed she owed Detective Nolan, too. The next time he came in the bakery, his large shot in the dark and scone would be on her. And maybe she'd take him out for a drink, too. He wasn't bad to look at, Will Nolan.

Once search and rescue and the sheriff had arrived, it had been controlled chaos. Everyone had been stuck at the chalet until morning light anyway, so they'd been hustled back into their rooms, tape placed across the outside of their doors by deputies that roamed the halls to make sure no one escaped before they could be questioned. It all seemed a little pointless to Sadie at that point. They already knew what had happened. Amalia confessed to the sheriff once the sedative Leo gave her wore off. She was kept in custody in the small room where Alex had told Sadie Adam's secret. She was considered a threat to herself, as well as others, so she had been constantly monitored.

Kendall and Kamari had decided, at Sadie's urging, to not risk their necks skiing unknown terrain in the dark during high avalanche danger and had bunked with her instead. The power came back on, more fuel having been pumped into the generator somehow, and they all enjoyed hot showers before piling into Sadie's bed, eating snacks Kendall had packed and exclaiming over everything that had happened.

Despite how exhausted Sadie had been, she didn't think she slept that night. The next morning at dawn a helicopter had arrived, and everyone was shuffled onto it to be evacuated after they were questioned in the great room, one by one.

When Sadie had faced Sheriff Wise, he'd thanked her for her service. She'd given him her full account. Amy's leggings, somehow stolen by Amalia. Steffy's planner, somehow snuck into Sadie's box of clothing. Adam's dark secret, but not that he might've killed Steffy had he had the chance. She would let Adam take that darkness to the grave with him, as she was sure it would haunt him forever. Being shot at outside. Being confronted upstairs by, as she now knew, Jon Jr, who'd been hiding in Steffy's bathroom in between bustling around trying to keep his mother from harming anyone else. Sadie's sting operation in the library. The dining room revelations.

He filled in some holes for her.

Amalia had stolen the leggings. She'd walked into Amy's room when she knew she was still in the great room and took them. She'd decided Steffy needed to die after hearing her talk about the Next Fashion Star episode so openly, and knew she needed to frame someone else. So she decided she'd frame Amy after the confrontation after dinner. She'd stuck the planner in Sadie's box of Glamarosa after Steffy's body had already been found, another way she'd tried to take the heat off of her and her darling son. It had been Jon Jr that had shot at them. Apparently, Amalia had been in the window above them, about to drop a brass buffalo sculpture on their heads, so Jon Jr had shot wildly to scare her off. The shot had hit the roof, jarring the icicles loose. After that, he'd decided he needed to come back in the house to keep an eye on her.

Sadie felt awful for him. His mother had killed his girlfriend, who he was in love with. But his girlfriend had been blackmailing his mother for years, bleeding their business dry with her demands for more prospects, more product, and more buy offs. Then he'd spent a frantic twelve hours trying to protect everyone from his mother, while trying to protect his mother as well, all while he was heartbroken and terrified. And Amalia had repaid him by telling Sadie that Jon Jr had killed Steffy. That poor kid.

When she'd been thoroughly questioned and debriefed, she was allowed to go. She gathered her things, kissed Flower the Rockchuck goodbye, and pointedly left every stitch of Glamarosa clothing in the suite. Dressed for the cold, she'd been escorted outside by a deputy she recognized from her bakery. White mocha and a slice of quiche, cold, so he could eat it by hand while he was driving. Of course she remembered his order but not his name. She'd been helped into the helicopter, seated next to Amy and Kendall and across from Gavin and Kamari, and they'd lifted off.

The sun had been blinding against the freshly fallen snow. The pilot banked, giving them the best view of the Tetons she'd ever seen in her life. Tears pricked her eyes. Amy gripped her hand. They'd survived. It was over.

Amy and Gavin didn't have anywhere to go, so Sadie had them come back to her house with her. An SUV was waiting for them at the helipad and drove them away. Sadie wondered how they'd get her van off the mountain. It might be there a long time. Repairing the landslide damage would take awhile. But that was a problem for future Sadie. She stopped asking questions, her head drooping on the drive.

When they'd arrived at her house, her parents had whisked her into her bedroom, her mom tucking her into bed like she was a child again. She presumed Amy and Gavin got the same treatment.

She'd slept like she'd never slept before. Deep, dreamless. She didn't dream of a woman with rainbow hair and big ambitions who had an idea someone else made successful so she grabbed onto the success however she could. But Sadie mourned, her, even now. She didn't know Steffy. She hadn't ever known her. Blackmailing people was wrong. But she hadn't deserved to die.

Now, Sadie took another sip of her margarita, studying the waves through her sunglasses. She'd been awoken by her mother three hours before her flight was supposed to leave, having slept all day. She'd said she wasn't going anymore, that she just wanted to rest, but Robin had produced a neck pillow and a sleep mask, and insisted she could sleep on the flight. And thank goodness she had. This. This was nice.

"Have you seen this?"

Amy plopped down in the chaise next to her and scooped

up one of Sadie's recently delivered nachos. She handed her a tablet with a news article pulled up.

GLAMAROSA SERVED WITH CLASS ACTION LAWSUIT AMIDST MURDER OF HIGH PROFILE SELLER BY FOUNDER

Sadie pulled a face. "Yikes."

"Yeah," Amy said, taking a sip of her own margarita. It turned out all that unreimbursed travel for Glamarosa had one perk—lots of airline miles and credit card points to spend. Amy had booked a last minute ticket to come along, and Sadie was glad for the company. Plus, Amy needed this, too.

Amy took the tablet back. "It's bad. I don't think they'll make it through this."

"I'm sorry for everyone involved. Honestly, Amy. I know this will cost a lot of people money."

"It will," Amy said solemnly. "And it will cost me too. But I'm out. I already hit cancel on my contract on the plane ride."

Sadie studied her. "How do you feel?"

Amy took a deep breath and surveyed the beach. "Free," she said finally.

They tipped their glasses, clinking them.

"To your new beginning," Sadie said.

"And to Steffy," Amy added.

"To Steffy." Sadie finished her drink, then stood. She was going to swim in the ocean. When she emerged, she was going to start thinking of a new beginning for her, too. She'd been so cranky the last few months, too caught up in everyone else getting everything she thought she wanted that she hadn't been able to appreciate what she already had. A business. A family. Amazing friends. A home she loved. A sweet dog. When she went home, she'd be looking at everything through new eyes.

She couldn't wait for what was next.

* * *

Thanks for reading! As an independent author, it means the world to me. Sadie and the gang next appear in my May novella, A Patchwork of Peril, available for FREE on my website: www.suepepperauthor.com

* * *

Book four, Tourist Trap Murder, publishes 9/27/22!

Author's Note

This book is a slight departure from my normal mysteries. It takes place over thirty-six hours in one location, your classic mansion murder mystery. It was a challenge to take Sadie Moose out of her diverse, quirky community and plop her into a setting without her normal sidekicks, but these characters came alive when I wrote them, and I hope you enjoyed it as much as I did. It's a little different in that there's no love scene either—try as I might, Adam was just too haunted to rekindle anything with Sadie, and Gavin's gay. Trust me, Gavin will stick around, he's too fun to not become a regular part of Sadie's crew. Maybe a love interest for Max? Hmm...

This was a very personal story for me to write. I left my steady government employment when my oldest kid was two for direct sales. It wasn't something I thought I would ever do, but the business, the promise of social media sales, the excitement, the travel...I fell hard. I left the direct sales biz several years ago now, and I look back at my time as a boss babe mostly with fondness. I met a lot of great people, helped a lot of women feel good about themselves, traveled a lot, and learned a lot about how to run a business—and how not to. But, I was lucky to get out

217

without enormous debt. I hold no grudge against those who do direct sales, but I hope they educate themselves on the business model and how it is often stacked against them. Yes, some people will have success, but 99% of people involved in multi-level marketing make no money or lose money (source: https://consumer.ftc.gov/articles/multi-level-marketing-businesses-pyramid-schemes#).

It's only lightly touched on in this book, but Jackson Hole is in the midst of a housing crisis. Many, many people, including my family, have been forced out of the community because of income inequality, a lack of affordable housing, and encroaching billionaires. I am donating a portion of the profits from this series to ShelterJH, an organization building grassroots and political power in Jackson Hole so that all community members can live where they work. I encourage you to give them your support and read through their policy platform. They have much better ideas on how to fix the problem than my works of fiction provide.

Acknowledgments

First, thank you, dear reader. This is my third published book, and I wouldn't have gotten to this point without your support. Thank you for reading, for rating and reviewing, for talking to your friends, for sharing on social media, and for your encouraging words in my inbox.

Second, thank you to all the boss babes out there. I hope you can laugh at this book if you see some of yourself in it, and know that I see and appreciate your hustle and your drive to make a difference for your family.

I am grateful, as always, to my family and friends for their support, particularly Whitney, Rachael, Kristen, Leah, and Jen. Y'all get me through the days.

Biggest thanks to my friend and beta reader, Lea. Thank you for loving Sadie as much as I do.

Thank you to my Advanced Reader team—you help get this book into the hands of more readers because of your thoughtful early reviews, and I appreciate you so much!

Thank you to my Sisters in Crime Guppy Chapter critique group partners, and thanks always for the support of my home chapter, Sisters in Crime Columbia River.

Thank you, husband, for your unwavering support during my boss babe era, and for your hand holding as I navigated the road out of it. Thank you for understanding when I must hole up and write, or when I zone out and frantically type book ideas into my phone in the middle of a conversation. I love you. You know when you start wearing shorts in the spring and I suddenly see your knees all the time? That's super sexy. Keep doing it.

Dearest children, I left my day job to be a boss babe for you, and I left boss babe-ing to be with you full time, and now I'm with you full time while I write full time, and I hope you know I have done all of this to maximize my time with you. You are my life's work. Mama loves you.

About the Author

Sue Pepper writes not so cozy mysteries in the Pacific Northwest where she lives with her two kids, fuzzy yellow dog, and real life action hero husband. A former resident of Jackson Hole, WY pushed out by the billionaire-caused housing crisis, she enjoys writing revenge and redemption for the fictional residents of her Jackson Hole Moose's Bakery Not So Cozy Mystery series, starting with her debut, Mountain Town Murder.

Find her online at www.suepepperauthor.com, Facebook, TikTok, and Instagram.

Also by Sue Pepper

Jackson Hole Moose's Bakery Not So Cozy Mystery Series

Available in print wherever books are sold, and in ebook form on Amazon and Kindle Unlimited:

Mountain Town Murder, #1

Hot Springs Murder, #2

Boss Babe Murder, #3

Tourist Trap Murder, #4

FREE interstitial short stories available at www. suepepperauthor.com/books:

Escape From the North Pole, #1.5

A Deadly Secret Admirer, #2.5

A Patchwork of Peril, #3.5